All the Rage

ALSO BY A. L. KENNEDY

FICTION

Night Geometry and the Garscadden Trains
Looking for the Possible Dance
Now That You're Back
So I Am Glad
Original Bliss
Everything You Need
Indelible Acts
Paradise
Day
What Becomes
The Blue Book

NON-FICTION

The Life and Death of Colonel Blimp
On Bullfighting
On Writing

All the Rage

A. L. Kennedy

New Harvest
Houghton Mifflin Harcourt
BOSTON • NEW YORK
2014

First U.S. edition

Copyright © 2014 by A. L. Kennedy

All rights reserved.

This edition published by special arrangement with Amazon Publishing

Amazon and the Amazon logo are trademarks
of Amazon.com, Inc., or its affiliates.

For information about permission to reproduce
selections from this book, go to www.apub.com.

www.hmhco.com

Published in Great Britain in 2014 by Random House

Library of Congress Cataloging-in-Publication Data
Kennedy, A. L.
[Short stories. Selections]
All the rage : stories / A. L. Kennedy.—First U.S. edition.
pages cm
ISBN 978-0-544-30704-9 (hardback)
I. Title.
PR6061.E5952A6 2014
823'.914—dc23
2013050974

Printed in the United States of America
DOC 10 9 8 7 6 5 4 3 2 1

For
V.D.B.
As Ever

CONTENTS

Late in Life

'Eating figs is different for girls.' She says this because she is being sexy for him to pass their time: standing in a queue and over-gently, over-carefully setting her lips to the fig, destroying it in an affectionate way. The round blush and kiss of the skin, the neat, small burden in her hand: she's aware it all makes for a less subtle show than he generally likes, but he's watching, he is now-and-then watching. And he gives her the quiet rise of what would be a smile if he allowed it. She knows this because she knows him and his habits and the way the colour in his eyes can deepen when he's glad, can be nearly purple with feeling glad when nothing else about him shows a heat of any kind.

He's quite frequently secretive. They have decided to like this about him. His love of hiding has nothing to do with her and should not be a worry – it dates from much earlier situations which were unpleasant. They agree that his varieties of absence are okay and usually endearing.

He nudges against her side, 'Shush.' This is a suggestion that she should hide, too.

She keeps on, though. 'There's one left, if you want.' This morning she'll be obvious for him and minutely brave.

She will undermine the calm of their nearest building-society branch with an outbreak of sex, or something not unlike it. 'Do you want?' What she wants is for other people to overhear her. Anyone, she feels safe to assume, can need the comfort of witnesses sometimes and to be remembered, on the record. 'I bought two.' At the moment, she would appreciate some comfort.

'Of course. You would.' His mouth flinching into happiness and then back. 'They're better in pairs. At least, we'd hope so.'

She bites. This doesn't honestly feel intimate any longer, only both interesting and wrong. If she were being accurate inside her little display, then she would simply warm and hold and be very kind to the figs. They would come to no harm. She would dote upon each of them in detail.

Instead, she is biting, eating.

Which may not seem arousing at all.

Maybe, from his point of view, she's acting out a threat. Not that he doesn't enjoy certain types of threat and the odder edges of sweet things. She has found she enjoys them with him – it's not that she has to pretend.

He nudges again, 'You couldn't have bought me an apple . . .?'

'You didn't ask.'

'I like apples.'

'I couldn't give you an apple – *woman inflicts apple on her partner* – it would be religious. Like a moral assault.'

They don't assault, not ever. That's a promise.

He nods solemnly, 'Leading me astray again.'

'No.'

As a couple, they are purely soft – hard ideas, but tender

application. Hardness was before, in all the years before they met, and they have declared an end to it.

'We should get a garden.' He stares past her and on into where he intends they should finally be. 'Then we'll grow apples. Figs, if you'd like. If the weather will allow. How about that?' With a brief touch to her neck, an enquiring contact.

It is not an impossible hope: they could soon plant a garden and shape it to be only theirs. After today – or before 5 p.m. tomorrow at the latest – she will have paid off her mortgage. Or rather, he will have paid off her mortgage, because he's *not short of cash* and had paid off his own decades ago, both of these circumstances slightly having to do with his age. Once they have sold her flat and his, they will move in together, more together than they currently are. They will buy – to be accurate, he will probably buy – a big new bed and sheets and everything fresh. They have planned this, pondered thread-counts and headboards, and they are sure they will sleep very beautifully once their requirements have been fulfilled. And they will also be there with each other and stay attractively awake. This means that when she reaches the head of the queue, she will be, in a way, receiving money for sexual reasons from an older man.

Hence the figs.

The money-for-sex thing feels mildly electric in the soles of her feet. She grins.

'What?' He kisses the top of her head. 'Why's the girl smiling? Or shouldn't I ask.' But he wants it out loud, she can tell: a further demonstration for the queue – *here's love, here's being desired and desiring, here's assured love.* Something else they share: a need to be as real as observers make them. When she hugs his arm, she can feel it tensing with his usual interior argument – that he'd like to be the unnoticed man, the invisible boy who is shy – that he'd like to burn and be uncovered and holding and licking where they stand, outrageous evidence. 'Shouldn't I ask?'

'You should always ask.' Still, she isn't absolutely clear what she should answer. 'My boy should always ask.' This quiet and for him, no one else.

She doesn't believe that when he chooses to be overt he's making a statement against decay: bridge in his top teeth, glasses, greying hair – greyed, to be truthful – thin at the crown. He's not any more needy than she is, she completely believes that and has said so.

'Then tell me why you're happy?' Shining with the answers he expects and with being content, a young kind of content.

The truth would be complicated, so she tells him, 'I was just thinking – what if there was a hold-up, robbers, guns?' And for a moment she has made him disappointed.

But then fully, plainly, he permits himself to be delighted. 'If there were guns I would save you.' There is no way to overestimate how fond he is of saving, of the thought that he will do her good.

So, once again, she's vindicated: she doesn't ever lie to him unless it's for the best.

Under her hand, his elbow twitches with a dream of motion. 'I'd have to rush in and defend you from the bullets – stand in their way.'

'No. I'd take a bullet for you.' This is a whole, uncomplicated truth. She would be murdered for his sake, if necessary.

'No, no.' He kisses this close beside her, nuzzles against their rush to be dead for each other. 'I'd be compelled to do the gentlemanly thing and lay down my life. It would be instinctive. Men of my generation can't help it. I would have to be terribly harmed and then expire.'

'In my arms?'

'Well, that would depend. If I was flinging myself at a gunman in a hail of hot lead I might not also be able to fall back and rest my head upon your shoulder.'

'Breast.'

'I'd be too poorly.' A dark and nice flicker in his look.

'It's traditional.'

'All right. Breast.' Saying this with enough focus to make himself swallow, pause. 'And if I failed to reach you, I would fail nobly and you would be impressed and you'd . . . then you'd probably – I don't know – you could lever me into position before I kicked off . . .'

They do this a lot: imagining dreadful scenarios. It is a kind of inoculation against the future. She makes sure she doesn't think of blood seeping through her blouse, or of the precise shape, warm and clever shape, the kind shape of his head, and how things would be if he wasn't breathing and his lips were still.

'What should I wear at your funeral?'

'Velvet. Vermilion. No. Crimson. If you wouldn't mind.'

'That's the same thing.'

'Not at all. Crimson's more blue and vermilion's more orange. I think . . . And crimson's spelled differently – it has a "c" in it. Like all the good things.'

'Vermilion Velvet sounds better.'

'Well, you're not wrong . . . I shall leave it up to you.'

'Okay.' She holds his hand. 'And will I jump into the grave and call your name and be devastated and inconsolable?'

'You'd spoil your dress.'

'I wouldn't care.'

'All right, then. I'll be in my box and I'll listen. As far as I'm able.'

'I will beat my tiny fists on the wood.'

'Thank you.'

They squeeze each other's fingers.

Ahead in the queue is a mother with a toddler daughter: all curls and frills and graded shades of pink. The girl has collected a leaf at some point, perhaps in her garden – the child's family may have a garden – or else during the walk to get here. Up until five minutes ago, the thing was a perfect little autumn in her hand, crisp-edged and tawny. The girl has loved it into splinters since then. She is currently staring at her palm and how it is dirty with veins and shreds, although she doesn't cry. Perhaps she has a philosophical turn of mind. Either that or she doesn't yet understand her loss.

He clears his throat, 'I've chosen the music.'

'For what?'

'For the wake. And the service.'

These occasions are only guesses and are so far away and distant and tiny that they can seem fun. And people of all ages joke about their funerals, pick tunes.

'You'll have Andrew Lloyd Webber and like it. Sea shanties round the coffin and then I'll play the spoons.'

'I'll come back and haunt you if you do. I'll come back and bite you.'

'Why else d'you think I'd do it?'

A student of the wandering sort shuffles past, his business concluded, and heads for the rest of the world. He seems exactly as bewildered as he did when he drifted up to make his enquiry.

Young men are easily confused, she's often thought this. They lack resources.

The building society is busy. There are nine strangers – including the toddler – straggled out between her and the end of her mortgage and then the probable garden with pre-existing, or easily purchased, trees.

Or maybe they'll change their minds and want decking with some pots – less work. Sit out of an evening and sip Martinis, daiquiris, home-made lemonade, and nobody doing their back in with mowing the lawn because there isn't one.

It doesn't do to over-prepare. She realises that it's good to let some mysteries remain.

Flower beds, or pots, or runner beans – it doesn't matter.

The woman ahead of her looks stressed and is holding a sheaf of ill-kempt papers. Whatever her problem is, it will take a while.

Monday lunchtime.

Predictably busy.

They should have known better.

There's the second fig to eat, yet – a distraction – except that it's his, intended for him. Not that she's asked if he likes figs. She made the assumption that he should because their tastes have been consistently in agreement right from their start.

It's something to give him, a fresh fig.

She doesn't want his money. She isn't truly accepting a

gift, she is agreeing that he has to save her and embracing that. Anything else would hurt him.

And she can't hurt him.

Without his intervention – although this isn't what it's about, or what they're about – her mortgage interest would tick and tick, asking £6.80 from her every day. Plus, her inadequate mortgage endowment is shrinking and shrinking, which loses her – by some unhappy coincidence – pretty much another £6.80 every day. In this area, and several others, it can seem that she is being punished for something unnamed: perhaps sins she is waiting to commit.

He has lately been very firm that she ought to get rid of her flat and she agrees. The place has become unreliable. There is something wrong, for example, with the roof. People move unaccountably in and out. Most mornings, when she checks the table in the hall, there is mail for entirely theoretical residents. Yesterday there was a letter addressed to 'Mr Basement'. She isn't aware of anyone using that name. Odd objects are left on the steps during the night: pieces of metal, old mops, plastic things that seem culinary, or else medical. There is a sense of illicit activities taking place. Meanwhile, and perhaps in response, the council has sent notices to say that odd objects will no longer be uplifted, or that they will not be uplifted so often as hitherto, or that they will be uplifted from other locations, as yet unclear.

'The council are turning off the street lights.' He does this occasionally: follows her thinking while it runs inside. 'This winter.'

'Really?' It's generally a thing to love: the way he is mixed in her thinking.

'Said so in the paper. To save money.'

'Can they do that?'

'Apparently.' He lifts her hand, which means he intends to kiss it and – *here* – does so, as if she were delicate fruit, the touch light as a breath and elongating. 'We needn't go out any more in the nights.' This hot between her knuckles, before he raises up his head and stares. 'We could stop in and have lanterns and a fire.' A blue and inquisitive stare. 'Do you think we'd enjoy that?'

'I've never seen you in firelight.' As if she has a list of ways in which she would like to see him: in dappled sunshine, or a CT scan, perhaps in evening dress, or else a movie of the 1930s with a railway platform underneath him and leather luggage and a hat. In school, at his first job, with his first love – so much she has missed.

'We'll make sure we have a fireplace. Garden and a fireplace. And then we'll get ourselves in firelight.'

'On a rug.'

'On a big rug.'

She can't deny this curiosity, this ache to have felt his earliest kiss, his potentially scared or possibly reckless activity when no one had ever been with him, or left him. Imagination is inadequate.

Asking him – *show me your past, let me have it* – could be misunderstood. She doesn't want him to be the man she's seen in photographs: Polaroid Christmases, dated clothes; that isn't who she loves, or who makes her undoubtedly satisfied. At night and on their daytime occasions – celebratory occasions, in his study with the paperwork jolted and spilling occasions – then he is always new, as smooth and new as teenage nonsense and summer running, as the best kinds of games. His pacing has maybe changed from what it was – he rolls up in waves and then back, has pauses – but his truth is only young and in the present tense. It is important that she keeps him absolutely sure of this.

If he doubts, she convinces him. That's how it is and will be.

And each time he's reassured, he draws in slightly closer.

'How are you surviving?'

'Okay. How about you?'

They are solicitous in balanced but not identical situations. She asks how he is during illnesses, if political news has upset him, if they have quarrelled. He asks after love-making, if she's tired, if they have quarrelled. They quarrel mainly at great speed, so they can move on to enquiries and holding and being held and can have nothing wrong any more. They lean on the rise and fall of their ribs when the shouting's done, old trouble in the press of breath. As a rule, they don't like being scared without each other, not even if each other is what scared them.

This morning hasn't been frightening, not quite. They spent it with each other in a lawyer's office, going through unspilled paperwork so that their lives will be coordinated and tidy from hereon in.

She called it *the document* instead of *the will*. This made matters slightly confusing and so she changed to *my document* and *your document* and eventually everyone – all three of them – was *document*ing.

Afterwards, business over, he kissed her in the street – a grey building at his back with a grubby doorway, and so she closed her eyes while they hugged and therefore spared herself the ugliness. He kisses very well. On that occasion, he was particularly fine.

Such an uncomfortable day, though. She would prefer if it were done.

But no need for worry.

No sense in making assumptions, or being bleak in advance.

There's no way to be certain of when anybody will leave.

After you.

In every doorway, without fail, he tells her.

That's what she wants.

After you.

Then at least she'd keep the whole rest of him and miss nothing else.

But he has to be the gentleman, can't help it.

No. After you.

Which wouldn't be right.

But neither is right.

Someone else having their apple trees, lighting unwatched fires.

And she isn't sure she'll manage, not in the end, doesn't see how she could, and she wishes she wasn't carrying this silly paper bag with the fig in it that she won't eat, can't eat. She wants to fold her arms, or put her hands in her pockets, she isn't clear which.

He settles his hand at the small of her back and then lets her swing and face him and see how he is weary and gently and sadly himself. 'Are you okay, though? Really?'

She doesn't ever lie to him unless it's for the best.

Baby Blue

What happened was that I got lost.

I swear to God.

I got mixed up and then was lost.

I didn't mean it. I didn't mean anything. I had, in fact, headed out on a jaunt, I might say if asked, so that I could skip meaning completely for a spell. I'd hopped on a plane to Over There, slipped out from the airport and into a brand-new Having A Break kind of city with hope in my heart for sustaining a speed consistently sufficient to outpace myself and every trace of significance.

There's no law against it.

Other than that, I had no intentions, not one in my head. I promise you. Truly.

And then in the hotel later that funny sleep caught me: the twitchy and messy unrest which comes after flight. A wrong sun was behind the curtains and my day had been knocked all westwards and stretched and my skin smelled frightened and of catering in confinement, bad catering, and also carried some harsh/sweet combination of scents that wasn't like me and wasn't something I could like. This despite having taken a bath as soon as I'd got to my room.

No one can win with long journeys: in every case, they precipitate bad bodily changes.

That's what I'd say. If asked.

That's what I'm saying.

I'd go on the record should I have to, although I won't. Why would I? To whom would this be of interest?

After the bath and the lying down and the discontent I woke up fifteen hours later raw-eyed. I'd got a headachy thirst as well – drank the whole big bottle of bedside mineral water, which I thought was free, but it turned out not.

What had roused me was the so, so quiet quietness – everywhere the broad silence which is the same in no matter which country and indicates snow. Even before I'd gone and checked the windows and worried I wasn't keeping up my pace, I already knew that, close around the outer walls, normality had been taken and this pale stasis was locked down in its place.

Same every time. One understands the symptoms, causes, and maybe refers internally for a moment to girlhood information about each individual flake being not quite the same as any another and having continually found this a source of disappointment when so many seem entirely the bloody same, just bland clumps and gobbets of cold. Not the miracles promised.

Because, of course, I continue to have an appetite for miracles promised, I stood and watched the whiteness dropping, fine and gentle, and wished them all well: not flakes, more a wavering dust, a disturbance barely visible in the blanked sky. This is the style of fall that doesn't seem it'll be a problem, but it's deceptive. The stuff doesn't stop and tenderly eats up your street, your views, and settles, and being out in it will make you end up cold – cold in the lungs – and still it keeps on and overwhelms and then the fun's gone.

There is usually fun at the start, I think. Snow makes the only wholesale change that human beings choose to tolerate. People embrace it.

We're an odd species, embracing ruined water, a gradually sifting possibility of disappearance. Some of us don't, I realise: those trying for specific ends and getting trapped away from them – making hospital trips, for example, contending with rural environments – residents of places held habitually under various things like winter, the effect of winter.

But city snowfalls conjure up simple delight. Often. More often than in the country. The older woman who comes and stays sometimes in the flat next door to mine, she adores it. Or, more properly, she demonstrates her adoration on behalf of someone else. That would be the best way to put it. *Oooh, la neige. Voilà. On peut faire les boules de neige.* One morning she was there on the front path with her bilingual grandkid looking up, or else with her she's-sodding-well-going-to-be-bilingual grandkid looking up – I don't know the woman, only to say *bonjour* to, and am unsure of her details – the grandkid looking and complete in wonder – beyond the *grand-mère* thing having been established, I can't recall exactly how, she's really a blank – this kid looking – pink outfit, so I presume a granddaughter, the nose visible and eyes, but not much else, which led to guessing – the bundled-cosy granddaughter looking up and widely about herself and breathless with the newly bright air and amazed by the strangeness lying and giving beneath her feet and the wonderful – *attention aux pieds!* – and the wonderful danger there, made fresh and lovely.

It was a great morning. I wouldn't swear to it having touched on fun, but it did feel clean. Or cleaned. Erased. Eradicated. I have an inordinate fondness for blank sheets.

Bright white and unbothered, that's what I like. A crisp domestic glare of cleanliness.

Love it.

Crave. I feel I can say I crave it.

I crave the potentially fraudulent kiss of fresh hotel sheets along limbs, even though the mattress beneath may be a nightmare of mites and skin cells, sweated into by strangers for several nasty reasons. It's a stupid thing to crave.

But I long for and choose to believe in the sharp linen. I allow it to give me confidence.

So here we have it.

Me standing by a foreign window on a valeted carpet, underfloor heat that's pleasing the bathmat, through in the bathroom where I'd have a shower soon – I had confidence.

Wash me in the water where you washed your dirty daughter and I shall be whiter than the snow.

I had a relative used to sing that.

Granddad. My grandfather sang it.

And, in addition, we have –

Kid standing and about to pitch in for a go at a laundered world. With her relative. Who maybe sings, perhaps French standards, favourites, Belgian show tunes, I couldn't say.

There's a type of confidence in both of them, too. There's noticeable faith.

Sod that, though.

It's all nonsense.

We can forget about the plane and the hotel.

They didn't happen.

Or they did, but they're not relevant where we are.

We could also get rid of the snow.

It has no place in the current narrative.

The winter-sports granny is true, absolutely, and numerous hotels and aeroplanes and weathers have been parts of my life, but they don't belong in the story I'm telling you.

This didn't happen abroad – this thing that happened – this parcel of things that happened – and this also didn't happen on the morning of the grandmother – *Vous parlez Francais? Un peu?* – and the obliterating sky. I shouldn't begin with leaving her behind and a walk to the bus stop beside the park and seeing the narrow balances of bleach-work along tree limbs, frosted trunks, the fountain halted.

There wasn't a fountain.

There never has been.

I don't know why I added it.

I want to describe my genuine circumstances on the occasion in question, but I can't.

I don't remember a bus stop, a bus, a journey of that kind. I usually drive. There would have been parking and, before that, the customary instances of discourtesy, bits of waiting – I'm sure there must have been – only I had no idea they might be of importance and paid them no heed.

But I was neither in an alien country, nor suffering unusual conditions.

That rubbish isn't true.

I did get lost. True.

I was raw-eyed. True.

I had passed a shallow night holding on against a memory of altitude and claustrophobia. Doesn't everyone? True.

I was tired. Contributing factor.

I might have thought briefly about the bread rolls served on aeroplanes and how they're incredibly cold, as if they've been delivered straight from the screaming sub-zero outside. Wherever they've been kept is somewhere unnatural, unbearable.

I might have thought that.

I do wander. In my thinking.

I have the impression that – on the day I might prefer to recall more entirely – I'd loitered in several places once I'd reached the city centre. There was a café, a health-food store with bargains offered on useless supplements, as endorsed by celebrity photos, none of which were remotely trustworthy or familiar.

That's probably the case. I can rely on myself about these points.

And then I went into somewhere that sold clothes that I would find despicable and therefore preoccupying as I pottered about, loathing bad seams and poor cuts and weird colours and cheering my mood with how horrible it might be if I were someone else with stridently different tastes, which would make anybody who saw me think I seemed dysfunctional and bizarre.

This was just a way to waste my time, not serious.

I was aware that, if I were someone else, I would have been pleased by the awful clothes and have bought something

I'd feel was charming, or else have put it in mind as a possibility for later, a treat, and – either way – I'd have gone home satisfied. I did realise that at the time.

I don't habitually hate or mock strangers and what they might like.

Unless I'm depressed.

Then I do it because it's cheering, but not too much and I get it over quickly.

So the proper preamble to my story is a blur of avoided purchasing and raised spirits.

And after that I wound up in another shop and began to make a moderate mistake.

I'm not ashamed.

I'd say that now.

It was something I walked into and couldn't control. Like the weather. It was like an unexpected stroll in snow.

If I'd been, I'll suggest this again, some other person with other likes and dislikes and not myself, then what was, in this case, unique for me might have been an already long-established and fond habit and no sweat. In someone only a little removed from myself, that could have been the case.

It must have been cold in the street. I believe that my hands were hurting in my pockets. They scolded. That memory's inflexible. So I can assume that I dodged indoors quite blindly to borrow a touch of warmth. I've been known to do such things before, particularly lately. I no longer concentrate as I once did.

The shop assistant was immediately – **Can I help you?** – right close at my elbow and her tone weird as she continued – **You were looking for something particular?** – which I wasn't – and she was asking me as if she was somehow a caring professional: not a doctor, or a nurse exactly, but maybe a dental hygienist, or a top-price hairdresser. She was dragging along this atmosphere of support and expertise which she leaned against me like a rolled-up carpet – second-hand, dusty – and there was a top note she put across most of her words to imply she was a friend I should confide in, girls together and ice cream this evening with crying and new lip gloss.

Lip gloss makes me feel constricted. As did she.

And wearing mascara's like peering through a fence. Make-up is what one does for others, isn't it? One goes to trouble.

One says things, if only to one's self, like *I have gone to trouble for you.*

As if it's a trip to be made on somebody's behalf.

I have gone to trouble for you, so you don't have to. I brought you back this souvenir, it's a small box of difficulties. You needn't unwrap them at once.

The gist of this was there in my head at the time – ideas being held – and there were other matters present, too, forming contours underneath the thinking, like knees underneath a bedspread. The knees have implications, but you don't have to deal with them, or not at once.

The assistant continued – insistent assistant – **For a special occasion?** – and I was, it must have seemed, drifting in an exploratory way along racks and shelves and display stands packed with choice. The lighting was unsubtle, so I found my surroundings rich in detail.

I was somewhere like a very big grocer's – **For yourself?** – a supermarket – times change and why be furtive, I suppose – a supermarket full of sex. Not sex. Devices engineered

– there was a lot of engineering – to mimic the effects of sex. Only devices – **For yourself?** – not costumes, or DVDs, or magazines, or books, or most of the things I'd expect to be in a sex shop, in as far as I'd never had expectations in that field and couldn't be sure, but must have surmised at some point. I surmise a great deal and at random. I did not intend to be there and yet there I was, nonetheless – **For yourself?** – and I had no answer. I'd halted in front of a bank of what were probably – definitely, now that I looked – fake vaginas and I couldn't answer – who would? – that, no, I intended to buy such a thing for someone else. Who? For whom? A female friend to whom I would suggest that their own was unhelpful? Or would I give one to a straight man as if he'd no chance of access to a real one? I'm sorry his girlfriend left him, never mind and here's this, which boils her down to her essentials? I'd want to imply that he felt these *were* her essentials and no wonder she left? Or would I foist one on a gay man? As what, a novelty letter box? Or I should deliver one to a lesbian as a hint she was sexually hopeless and ought to make do. This is – **For yourself?** – an impossible enquiry. Yes, for myself and I will give it to my partner because I want a rest? Or am I lacking? Or am I supposed to be gay and irreversibly solitary? Or have I discovered that mine doesn't work any more?

I attempted a smile that intended to seem well informed and relaxed. The assistant wore a name badge which called her Mandy, although I couldn't accept that as likely.

I adjusted my smile, broadened its dimensions.

I didn't want Mandy, or whoever she was, to imagine that I had no sense of fun.

Fun is important.

I constructed a small and intentionally visible idea of myself as someone with numerous options and a wide-ranging social circle. I folded my arms and moved on with purpose and as if I had no need of guidance – **Oh, then these** – Mandy wouldn't let me be – **These are wonderful** – I rounded the end of the aisle with her in tow and announcing – **They really are** – as she reached for a favoured item, being factual, not salacious – **Things have moved on** – and she offers me what things have moved on to from among the gathered ranks of more and less sci-fi imitation penises.

It didn't look – *thank you* – very much like a penis at all. Mandy had judged me – *thanks* – over to my left were obsessively anatomical offerings – *thanks* – Mandy had judged I would favour something impressionistic. Vague. Elegant lines. Inhuman.

I had the air, then, of someone who might wish to redesign their partner.

Thank you.

To love and despise simultaneously – Mandy assumed I was capable of that.

Thanks.

Clever Mandy.

Thank you – trying to – *really, thanks* – get rid of her with gratitude and taking the package – mainly a clear plastic bubble for ease of inspection – *thanks now, yes* – and my aim was to shift off to the back of the place, ditch the thing and leave.

Actually, not-so-clever Mandy.

I don't love and despise. That wouldn't be clear in my face, not to someone who knew me, because it isn't factual.

Mandy is a bad judge of character.

I love and resent.

Everyone does that, it's impossible to avoid. The real experience of love is of having unreasonably lost all shelter. There are wonderful additional elements in love apart from that, factors and truths which demand more than affection, which require worship of sorts, but there is, there really is, that initial loss. Sudden. And you cling to whoever is with you for sheer safety, beyond anything else. You cling to whoever has robbed you and they cling back because they are equally naked – you have stripped them to their blood. They are your responsibility, frail and skinless. It can't be helped.

I hurried from Mandy.

I rushed to the extent that I could rush without suggesting unseemly desire to acquire some further contraption with which to astonish my privacy.

The far wall of the shop offered objects that weren't coat hooks, that wouldn't enable arthritic hands to open tricky jars, that couldn't be used for games of hoopla, even though they were unwieldy, even though they were unlikely, even though the human pelvis could never accommodate them as an internal feature and they were therefore unfit for their stated purpose.

All these wild attempts at satisfaction, these declarations of absurd need.

Chocolate-flavoured condoms. They had chocolate-flavoured condoms.

You like penises, you like chocolate, why not both?

There were many *whys* for *not both*. For many reasons, my opinion was in favour of *not both*.

If I like penises, might I not be assumed to hope the flavour of a penis will be penis, which is to say not too much of a flavour, ideally just this subtle, unflavoured pleasantness and that isn't a problem, how could that be a problem? I don't feel my experience of oral sex is intended to be primarily culinary.

Unless is it? Have I got this wrong? Is it not about love, about knowing and being known? Is it – I can get confused – perfectly reasonable in that, or any other, context to insist, to appear to insist, to act in such a way that I'd be insisting *your penis is inadequate and ought at least to taste of chocolate to compensate, so here you go and roll on one of these?*

Am I being over-sensitive? Am I mistaken in thinking that when I touch the man I love, no matter where I touch the man I love, in no matter what way I touch the man I love, then the point is that I'm touching him and it's love and the whole of him is him and I am happy with the whole of him and my aim is to produce an increase of happiness in both parties and where he is tender I will be tender because that would be only right and the best and finest thing and sweet to my soul and lips in tender places can be tender. Even in the rush and stroke of the moment, it's only simple, only tenderness.

Nothing else would be required.

Something else would be an insult.

I wanted to explain this, because it was important, but nobody I'd want to hear me was there to listen.

I peered from behind the hoopla section until Mandy had pounced on another woman and led her away. They were chatting back and forth as I supposed they were intended to, taking advantage of a female-friendly emporium and an informative and unembarrassed ethos and I didn't care about my position per se, but it still made me angry, nevertheless.

Although this was a setting unsuitable for rage.

And anger is always the second emotion, something else having always been there first.

I wish I'd never learned that.

Fear and pain being the most usual precursors.

I would rather not notice the signals that prove I've been hurt or frightened.

Nothing else for you today? – I couldn't quite understand how Mandy had ambushed me again. I'd been heading to the penis area to abandon mine – it was not mine, but was burdensome enough by then to be taken personally – and I'd hoped to be free soon, but there she was – **Ready?** – the pert and relentlessly outgoing and dreadfully helpful Mandy. **I'll take you across to the cash desk.** As if I was an invalid, imbecile, had never visited a shop.

I could see the cash desk. I did not wish to visit the cash desk. I did very much wish to leave.

The easiest option was simply to buy the thing.

Buy it and get out.

We're a Canadian company. I don't know why I had to be told this. **We do things the Canadian Way.** Inexplicable. The young man at the till – I am now of an age, apparently, when the men at tills in sex shops will seem perceptibly young – created some kind of merry personal tension with Mandy. His name badge announced **John**. Mandy and John eyed each other across me as if they were a remarkably blasé couple, looking forward to an evening of not sex.

John – **We like you to be happy** – dextrously unpacked

the penis and – **I'll pop these in** – did indeed pop batteries – several – inside it before scooping one of my hands off the counter and setting the already-thrumming thing across my palm. Mandy smiled and took over – **There we go** – adjusted the settings up up up and down down down. This being of no use to me.

I had not intended to stand in public holding an electric penis while it performed keenly, then gently, then sluggishly, then not.

This way you know it works and is what you want.

John repacked it – **More batteries?** – Mandy was meanwhile incredibly – in the sense of being unbelievably – pleased by this whole turn of events – **We have a deal on batteries.**

I threw everything away once I got outside.

And the entire palaver didn't matter, was unimportant.

I know.

There may be no Canadian Way and perhaps they were only a couple with a kink working through it together in a ludicrously ideal location. Or they were making a joke of me. I don't care about them.

Except that they were more strangers intruding and I am tired of that.

I am so tired. Contributing factor.

I go to bed and hope for fifteen hours uninterrupted and they don't arrive in the same way that there is no snow, or no fun in snow, or no miracle about it.

I get so angry.

Uninterrupted fury is a constant.

It flickers near and far, but stays with me beneath superficial variations.

Which is why this preposterous shop – this preposterous

story about this preposterous shop, preposterous strangers – it's why I hold them tight.

I hold them until I sweat with holding and I can have faith there is something in my arms, against my arms.

I hold on until I have confidence again in the truth of sweet and voluntary touch.

Even in its absence I can believe. That's what belief is all about – it cannot exist without absence.

Honestly.

I need no substitutes or replacements.

I am lost, but not that lost.

I can subsist on faith.

It seals me away from remembering the afternoon not so far before the shop. Hospital trip – latest hospital trip – mild outside, but the corridors snowy, as if filled with bruised snow – past the doorways and in and undress and smell wrong and like a stranger and wait in the bedroom – wear the gown provided and get into the bed – they wheel me onwards using the bed once I am dressed as someone other than myself – the wide elevator yawning and sluicing me down to the theatre level – chat with the orderly – politeness – I'm paying – shame the public system doesn't work – I pay for that, too – but I pay more for this because then I'm less frightened, then I can think I'm doing something. I am my priority and contain the sum total of my hope. There are smiles as I go, propelled under the lights, and then come the intrusions and I am brave – just looking around to check the theatre, the monitor, the other equipment – I produce jokes, things that have moved on from jokes – and I'd rather not have the sedative and so get discomfort instead, not pain precisely – severe to moderate discomfort – I am very brave – I say this to myself – there being nobody about who is better informed.

Well done. You are being brave.

But when I said *you*, I meant *me*.

That was understood.

You weren't there.

This story's position is unequivocal on that: your absence.

You weren't there.

You aren't there.

You aren't here.

Not your fault, I know.

It's because I left you.

I have gone to trouble for you, so you don't have to.

Left as if I was going on a jaunt to Over There and gave you no part of the story about the bad bodily changes and the nothing much that anyone can do.

No confessions, no lip gloss and crying.

I'm not in the mood.

No longer being a woman, not a complete woman, not comfortable and me, not as far as I can tell, since they've taken what they had to away. More may be removed on future occasions. Things moving on while I fail to keep pace.

That's why the shop annoyed me.

Mandy.

Mandy and her shop selling everything unnecessary.

She hadn't got a clue.

She'd never lain down with the neat snug of you and held your full attention – cooling skin and being in the afterwards of us – the afterwards being really the destination – the afterwards being the requested now – she'd never eased fingers by your cheek, brushed along your jaw inside a new quiet, just touching and peace and us – she'd no idea.

She didn't understand reality.

She hadn't kissed you when you taste of the most excellent stories, perfect in my mouth.

I wish I could tell you about her.

I wish I could give you this story.

I can't, though.

I've gone to trouble without you, because what else could I do? I'm the one who took away your shelter, so I can't bring trouble back to you, I can't drag down the cold to hurt you. It has become necessary to be lost.

If I could see you, I would say this.

I miss you very much.

Because It's a Wednesday

B ecause it's a Wednesday, he's shagging Carmen.
Grotesquely unlikely name for a cleaning woman, Carmen. It doesn't even suit her as a person – entirely inappropriate, in fact. As is the shagging, of course. I am her employer – professional relationship, position of trust and so forth – I should be more restrained.

Not that a shag might not indicate trust.

I could argue that, to a degree, I am really confirming some level of interpersonal détente.

It had started, the shagging, when Philip's office hours were cut. Inadequate warning and then he's semi-permanently Working From Home in the flat – emailing, drafting and whatnot – bit of a shock – while Carmen's there setting his rooms to rights – polishing, ironing, folding, making his good order better and getting the place to smell of nowhere, or else like a well-maintained leisure centre, café, meeting room, a neutral space.

Which is what I request – no trace of my having been here, no spillages, no confusions, no scent beyond fresh linen, dry heat. **Impersonal.** People say that as if it's a bad word when it's fundamentally pleasant and light and unstressful.

Fifth new apartment in six years – third city, third country – sustaining that level of movement, you want to feel unrestricted, stay painless, be able to slip in and out.

No pun *intended.*

Christ!

Old bloke shagging the help, and cracking interior single entendres.

That's a bit desperate.

He stares at his hands where they're gripping her waist. Old man's hands he has now.

How did they happen? When? Where was I?

They give the impression he's wearing ill-fitting gloves, gloves with baggy knuckles. And big, ribbed, spadey finger-nails – a vulnerability about them.

And pale, pale, pale.

Carmen is wearing the pink-and-white-striped blouse today, which is his second favourite. His favourite is the green, the one she was wearing when they first shagged, when she stood up and made her move once they'd finished their cup of tea with the chocolate biscuits. This ritual they'd fallen into – there they would sit, eating these biscuits with bad, cheap chocolate on top and sharing a silent cup of tea at roughly, regularly, twelve o'clock. With no provocation, on that one particular afternoon – at 12.25, or so – she'd stood up and leaned against the kitchen counter, given him a slightly complicated look and then raised her skirt.

Not enticing, not particularly sexual, but unmistakably a request.

She doesn't have very good English – not at home in it – probably thought a gesture would be more effective.

Which it was.

No idea what she actually speaks inside her head, what her language is.

Should ask to see her passport, find out.

International, me – fluent in several places, but it's English that's the big one, is dominant.

Which is a happy happenstance.

She was wearing white knickers – always does – dull from too much washing, unadorned, but somehow girlish. Surprising.

Odd when you suddenly realise that somewhere in your mind you have made an assumption about someone's underwear, even though you have at no point imagined – not even considered – that you will see it, or touch it, or pull it down and have a shag.

Shag.

She is very definitely a shag.

This isn't *fucking*, Phil's not of an age any more to *fuck*. He lacks the energy and what he thinks of as the necessary edge. And Carmen, being plain, is not *fucking* material – he has to be truthful and truly she is not.

And we are absolutely not **making love**.

Phil has no patience for the expression. He feels it suggests that love can be fabricated like scaffolding or a hull, or that it might be forced inside a collaborator, injected, sweated into life. He does not believe this to be the case.

Philip and Carmen *shag*.

A dogword, dogged – something comfy and tousled,

*sturdy, reliable, warm-muzzled, panting. You can meet its
eyes and know just what you'll get. Uncomplicated.*

She's bent over one of his kitchen chairs – the knickers
and tights rumpled down to her shins, skirt rolled – lately
she has let him do this, has allowed him to partly roll and
partly fold it out of their way. He imagines this is to save
unnecessary creasing. There's a mild blush spreading on her
buttocks.

Mustn't think of that, though, or I'll come too fast.

Philip is picturing railway lines and sidings, cuttings, the
approach to his current city's largest terminus: overheard
wires and power ducts, channels, signals, warning signs,
tracks shining down to disappearing points – the naked
workings of transportation, their clarity – it calms him.

He crouches against and beneath her, up her, paces
himself to a steady *digdigdig.*

Dogdogdog.

Shagshagshag.

Although he needn't, he is being courteous. There absolutely is no point in holding back – she never seems to come
herself, never attempts an explanation of why they do this, or
what she might want. Even so, he does very often try to please
her, to break a noise from her beyond the loudish rhythm of
her breath. He has called her by name on a few occasions –
Carmen – but she hasn't answered, hasn't turned her head.

Although he guesses this is not what she prefers, he tends
to shag her from behind, purely because when he faces her
he can't avoid being aware that she doesn't smile, avoids
kissing, looks beyond his shoulder throughout as if she were
puzzled by some detail, or attempting to recall an itinerant
fact.

And always in the kitchen.
Domestic servant, knows her place.
Oh.
Shouldn't think of that, either. Anything hierarchical gets too horny.

He'd felt quite peculiar afterwards, on that initial afternoon – chilled and thirsty and curious, possibly affronted, but also sinking a touch into a kind of softness, a gratitude – it had been a while, after all. He'd briefly considered taking her to bed and starting again, pretending they had some meaning for each other. But Carmen had only released him, dressed herself, cleared the tea things, left.

He did wonder if she'd be back, but the following Wednesday she appeared at nine, the same as usual – only now the extra half-hour added for the shag.

It had been difficult to know if he should pay her more – he was, clearly, increasing her workload, in a sense, but he'd guessed any offers of extra cash would be distasteful. For a while, he'd left small gifts beside her tea mug. She ignored them. He'd begun conversations she either wouldn't or couldn't finish, had reached out to pat her arm when she was passing, had aimed to create an atmosphere of, if not affection, then positive regard, but she seemed to dislike this and as a result he had taken to rushing a roll of notes at her when the month ended and being vague about how much he genuinely owed, overestimating as if by accident.

I can afford it. Afford her.
Oh.
Not yet, though.
Oh.
One day she'll make me think of additional vowels.

Meanwhile, divert myself.

Affording.

Comforts.

Luxuries.

Pleasant situations.

Yes. Right up to the walls I am most pleasantly situated and living well within my means, living well completely.

When he'd viewed it, the flat was already exhaustively furnished and equipped – carpets, bed sheets, towels, ornaments, pictures, cutlery, pans, reading glasses, candles, lampshades, soap – as if the owners had left on holiday and had asked him to stay and take care of their belongings. Generously vacant for him – sign the inventory and he was home.

Mine.

My floor, my wall, my window, my view.

Outside it's easing into spring. Blossom shivers in the tall, haphazard trees and young light is being kind to the buildings opposite, the thin lane that runs beside them.

Foxes in that lane at night. I can hear them. Foxes in the city, and rabbits and hawks – the countryside's cleaned, it's shriven – but here there's hunting day and night. There are screams – exactly like women. In the morning I see traces.

He can feel heat running at the backs of his legs, the strain of the end on its way and he studies the shop fronts, clings to them for a beat and a beat and a beat.

Flower shop – no one goes in it, except for funerals, not properly an area for flowers, not yet. Refurbished café – one of those chains. Twenty-four-hour grocer's and off-licence. Tobacconist. Chemist. Somewhere that's still empty – whitewashed windows, dust.

He can see from the broad, slanted outlines left on the sandstone that the business was called *Zumzum* – silly name – typical.

No way of knowing what they sold, probably fancy cloth, or gold jewellery, maybe weird little cubic sweets, the kinds of stuff those people liked.

Butcher's still here from the old days. New management, naturally. Sausages, pork pies, nice bit of steak for the weekend – have to support your local butcher. Funny lettering over the door from when it was different, stocked different meat. Cheap paint, it'll fade.

Transitional areas. Reclamations. They start off unsteady, blanks where you wouldn't expect them, oddities, reminders, and then in the end, everything fades. You get a new community. Peace.

And, before the disruptions settle and the fresh life grows, you can roll in and get a cheap flat with all the trimmings.

My street, this is – in my neighbourhood – my house in my street in my neighbourhood.

And my view, my window, my wall, my floor, my chair, my shag.

My shag.

Oh.

My shag.

Oh.

Possession.

Oh.

Does the trick.

Oh.

Quite.

Phil draws himself away from her, removes the condom.
Can't be too careful.

He's pressed her forward and her blouse has ridden up.
For a moment he has to stare at the scarring on her back
– purplish/red and swollen. Then she straightens, hides it.
He's never been able to see the whole of it.

Burning.

Beating.

Some wrongness.

Some wrong act.

He bins his little parcel of semen, the tepid crush of
what he's left, and adjusts himself, clears his throat. He's
sticky, needs a shower and maybe an aspirin, but he can't
enjoy either until Carmen's gone, in case he gives offence.
This means he can only loiter and wait for his pulse to dim,
keep his hands from rising to his face, because they will
smell of activities and people, needs, heats.

By the far table leg he notices there are crumbs – he
must have dropped a sizeable piece of biscuit and then
trampled it into a mess while he was busied.

Dirty old man.

He inspects the bottom of his shoe – more biscuit.

Tsk.

That being the noise of crushed biscuit.

When she turns, respectable again, he points to the mess
and notices what could be a mild warmth in her expression,
a certain friendliness towards the idea of sweeping. Before
she goes for the pan and brush, she upends both the shagging
chair and Philip's ordinary chair and rests them on the table.

He's seen it before, of course – Carmen, too. Someone
with a clear, dark hand has inked a surname and a date on

the underside of each seat. There is a liquid, foreign taste about the script, not unattractive. Philip knows – having, late one night, eventually checked all his furniture – that the same date and name have been written on the back of his dresser, the headboard of his bed, under his sofa, somewhere on every chair, beneath lamp stands, inside cupboards where the door frames make a shadow. He is almost, almost, almost surrounded by a multiplicity of records, marks.

In the spring of last year.

Before they left.

Some morning, probably morning – early hours most suitable for clearing out.

Blossoms through the window and closed shops.

Making a good order better for everyone.

Goodbye. Goodbye. Goodbye.

Didn't even take their nail clippers, or the Thermos flask.

How strange it must have been to be so unimpeded. Like falling.

Carmen tidies round him, then quietly empties the tea leaves out of the pot and – as it happens – probably on to the condom.

She rights the chairs and he sits, a little light-headed. She washes the crockery which was here when he arrived and dries it with the tea towel which was rolled neatly with some others in a drawer – scenes of village life, British sea birds, common knots, blue-and-white checks, red-and-white checks, plain blue.

Once she's done, Carmen walks to stand close at his side, eases her scrubbed and tidy fingers inside his jacket, finds his pocket and takes out his comb, his own personal comb.

He exhales, with the intention that she will feel it.

And then he lets her.

He lets her comb his hair – run the little teeth back from his forehead, over his temples, smooth him from his hairline to his nape, and he drops his face forward and nods, indicating that she should continue and sometimes they do this for twenty minutes, for half an hour, or until he forgets, until he fades, until he's clarified.

It helps.

It definitely helps.

These Small Pieces

How it came to be that he ended up here was among the many mysteries. He'd been following – or not quite, because how could he? – this guy, probably a guy, on a scooter. Dandy cream-and-red Vespa and somebody riding it wearing a cream cut-off raincoat and cream helmet – there'd been a theme going on, cream theme – and it had drawn his eye and he'd ambled along in the wake of the stylish scooterist, kept walking on inside this persisting slipstream of mild coolness, the impression of someone else's sorted life gently peppering his face, uncaring. And once he'd been tempted away from his customary track, it was then apparently much more than possible for him to find that he'd gone and sat himself down in a church.

Bloody Christmas.

They got you through the door with Christmas.

The whole of the city centre was already mental because this was the morning of the Santa Dash – runners in cheap felt Santa get-ups jogging about the Sunday streets and ruining the magic for any children they happened to pass. He'd seen this girl, all of her nothing but a sudden shine and full of big breaths and about to call out, or laugh, or just make some personal noise of completed joy, because there, as far as she could tell, was Santa Claus – truly and in person Santa Claus – pelting up towards her on Nike trainers. Good news all round. Only then behind that Santa came fifteen other bastard Santas – a sense of feral pursuit in their demeanour, you might almost say – and you could entirely hear the kid's heart breaking – *tump, tump* – and watch the sink in her chest beneath the quilted anorak – mauve and with a fur trim and almost new, she clearly had attentive parents – as she works out, one ugly piece at a time, that the reindeer and chimney stuff were utterly some revolting scam and that people lie and fine ideas are better left unrealised. Premature adults were being created throughout two postcodes and this would continue at least until lunchtime.

So he'd gone inside to get away from *tump, tump*.

His arrival at this location was less about the scooter, then, and more about fleeing epidemic grief.

That and the door had been open and a jolly sign right by it announcing the high probability of Christmas carols as if they were mince pies and not so much religious as just sweet and, peering past the threshold, he'd seen candles ranged out in the season's proper colours and atmosphere music was being provided: posh and twiddly ladders of festive notes making heavenward scampers and proving the organist was both classy and keen to demonstrate the fact. And in most directions also was a sense of healthy families, handshakes, gathering, a comfortable knowledge shared.

The combination of elements had caused him to stride in, as if belonging, and to *good-morning* nod at one, two, three strangers who *good-morning* nodded back, probably more as a reflex than as a comradely response, because they afterwards seemed bewildered and looked away.

He'd sat himself near an edge, the leftward extremity of the forthcoming events. This wasn't because he felt out of it or unclean: rather, he'd spotted a radiator that he could lean beside. The church being one of the cold traditional stone and arching roof-beam type – picturesque and making its point with flair – he knew he'd get chilly if he fitted himself in the wide-open midst.

Before he settled, he'd neither dipped his finger in the magic water, nor dipped his respect to the watching mind hung up above the magic altar. He'd not even slotted a glance along the central aisle to where, no doubt, the flame of forever was burning and where, no doubt, the blood of forever was moulded, recorded, elevated, shown flowing to indicate the likelihood of sympathy between the small and the omnipotent – *tump, tump: we've each been disappointed in the heart*. No doubt.

It seemed no one had disapproved of his laxity. It seemed no one had noticed.

Hi, I'm Sandy. Hi, I'm Douglas. Hi, I'm Martin, Richard, Nigel. He tried on the names he might use while he was here, could offer to fellow congregants in the drift and scuffle at proceedings' close. Or else he might murmur as he filed out – *lovelysingingsuchagiftitwasthankyou* – past the master of the ceremonies – *I'm Adrian.*

No, Douglas would be best. Douglas felt comfortable.

For some reason, Douglas would rather his actual name didn't have to be heard at present and in these surroundings.

I'm Lawrence. I'm Steve and I'm visiting from out of town. I work in IT. Actually, I'm a naval architect.

Or he could leave without an explanation.

Doug, Doug Fordyce. I have been disappointed in my heart.

He would be Douglas, or sometimes Doug. Doug, who was here on the way to somewhere, at the limit of everything, and maybe unable to tell wrong from right without assistance. That was the assumption in this place, that his morality was not inherent for him. Poor Douglas. He needed help.

Although it could be, in his finer moments, that Douglas did okay. Blessing him might be an imposition and he might, in actuality, already walk along narrow paths of peace and cleanliness and have been born for nothing else. You never knew with Douglas.

The bell sounding to bid them stand, Doug was up and swaying from heel to toe with perhaps anticipation and perhaps unease. A welcome, quite sincere, was issued and then a civilian gave the initial reading, which spoke of God commanding Abraham to murder Isaac.

'Kill your son for me.'

'All right, then.'

Which was a bit of a weird choice, given the season and the presence of youngsters, although there was, Doug supposed, the happy ending after the period of mountain-climbing and suspense.

'On you come, then Isaac. We're there. Sorry again and all that. God's orders.'

'Thanks for letting me get my breath back.'

'Well, that won't be permanent.'

'What?'

'Least I could do, son – give you a bit of a pause. If there was any other option . . .'

'No, it's fine. I'll be fine. Not to fret.'

And then God sweeping in with, '*ABRAHAM, ARE YOU OUT OF YOUR MIND? OF COURSE DON'T DO IT. WHY WOULD I ASK YOU TO DO IT?*'

'You did ask me to do it.'

'*I WASN'T SERIOUS.*'

'I've a knife at my son's throat, we're both exhausted and you're not serious. What's he going to think of me hereafter?'

'It's fine, Dad, I said.'

'I cut him a bit. Look. Shaky hands and that.'

'I didn't feel it.'

'He'll not be taking voluntary country strolls with me now, God, will he? He'll be watching the cutlery at mealtimes is what he'll be doing. Asking me to kill my son . . .'

WELL, YOU'LL DO IT TO ME LATER.

'What?'

AND I'LL LET YOU.

'Sometimes, honest to God, God, I've got no idea what you're on about. I'm not sure that you do, either.'

LEAVE ME BE.

'I'm fine, Dad. I'm fine, God.'

DON'T BE RIDICULOUS, OF COURSE YOU'RE NOT FINE AND DON'T CONTRADICT ME. I KNOW EXACTLY HOW YOU ARE. AND YOU DID FEEL IT.

When Doug thought about it, he was pretty quickly sure – as usual – that no one should think about it, no one should consider anything to do with God. Drowning everyone and then inventing rainbows to make up for any inconvenience and *THIS SHALL BE A SIGN THAT I WON'T DROWN THE WHOLE SAD PACK OF YOU AGAIN WHEN I FEEL LIKE* and then Job being given it hard from every possible direction to basically settle a bet; the Bible did tend to show that God could not be relied upon for much, would turn your wife into a pillar of condiment, would tempt you, plague you, write on your wall, send you dreams that would leave reality tasteless for you, grey-bland.

Doug let his attention romp about a while to save deeper confusions and the outbreak of resentment.

Set in a niche on the opposite side of the church to his own was a statue of God's mother, who bore God's son – and who was therefore God's wife as well, God help her and he did – with only the minimum of warning.

Blue cloak and the star-scattered halo, one foot pressing definitively on a willing, or shocked, or semi-conscious snake.

First carol.

What he came for, the singing. That was his sole aim.

Say what you like about Doug, he was a reckless singer. Out of practice and not able for the higher notes – because how long is it really since he's sung anything – but he rattles his voice and efforts in amongst the comingbacktohim words and does his utmost with head up and slightly the manner of the child he could have been, had he ever existed. Decades ago, Douglas could have been prone to white aches of passion for an unhuman love and the hope of bigwinged-warmwinged angels with serious eyes and the glow of a wise and approachable baby, laid out amongst animals and presents, like one more of both at once when animals and presents were the greatest things.

He remembered feeling that kids always understood kids. And Doug perhaps shared the common opinion that you could rely on the golden baby to see your side of it. By spring, the tender nipper would have grown up scary, harmed, and that would be totally down to you. He would be an elaborate reproach. It was only at Christmas that he was okay.

The subsequent reading stepped back within more prudent limits – Mary getting her tidings and even another baby on the way to another mother, a mother without hope, and NOTHING WILL BE IMPOSSIBLE WITH GOD, which might be as much a threat as any type of promise. There should be a line between impossible and possible, there shouldn't be crossing and seeping, elsewise the world becomes a trick and not a place, not a home. This was Doug's opinion.

A lullaby passed and then an anthem, familiar.

The Mary statue over the way remained unimpressed, God-baby in the crook of her arm, but her eyes not towards it – no, both of them were fixing on the middle distance and matters incomprehensible to most.

Wise men arrived and were foolish and spoke, as ever, incautiously and innocents were ended and shepherds had their naked sky torn across by heralds, a night full of terror and din and this need to travel. In Doug's, or someone's, head the passages tumbled together until they were refined into one lunchtime at primary school – somebody's authentic recollection – when a boy spoke up loud and talked about the manger. Gentle word, manger. He took it to be a kind of cradle.

The boy remained a boy for only the usual period. Then he was, as recommended, put away with the other childish things.

And Mary set her foot over the snake, because she

could and because it was Sin and she was not. And in the Original Garden, deep at the start of ourselves, Eve was led astray by the serpent and, that so long time afterwards, Mary wasn't. And plainly the snake is, more properly, the bad maleness of man, the writhing soft-hard wickedness he carries ahead of him into his life, the heat he goes astray with. Mary stamps on it. *Bad boy* and she stamps it flat.

She reminds the more thoughtful, the put-away boys, that the beast was only cursed to go on its belly after it gave man and woman the knowledge of how they were shaped to fit each other sweetly and, furthermore, shaped for wide, mad catalogues of other pleasure. This meant that, before the curse, there were legs maybe, legs and arms and elbows maybe, the presence of some other, unrecorded man in Eden maybe, one who knew what he was all about and who spread the word and then was reduced to his essence in animal form: side-winding lust with a tongue in flickers and hard eyes.

Doug flinched somewhere at the sharp idea of it. He was quite sensitive, Doug.

I MADE YOU AND HELL MEND YOU.

Which was hardly fair.

DID I SAY IT WOULD BE?

And now another tune washed over him from childhood and shook loose something, nothing, some emptiness that wanted to be filled with apples and angels and promises and releases from sacrifice.

This was customary; you wanted it in a Christmas service: an opportunity to weep.

Douglas, or whoever, shivered and the snag and heave

and braveness in his breath surprised him. Wipe at the eyes
when he sat and no shame about it.

Before this lifting up of prayers started, the guy with
the lectern, quiet and sincere, deliberately named the anxious
and lonely and fearful and so forth.

He took pains to make his audience aware of them.

He was beseeching.

His audience was beseeching.

Douglas was beseeching with them, he couldn't avoid
it, and was hurt beneath his ribs from the effort, the
wholesale striving for others' sake.

No thoughtful child, no watching mind, could say
they didn't care or hadn't asked, considered feasible
improvements.

And then here is the final carol coming, designed as a
crescendo, the triumph of being born as solid in the music
as the triumph of refusing to be dead – lower harmonies
thrumming in the floor, as if hell is dancing and not so bad,
nowhere and nothing so bad as the man who isn't Douglas,
as the put-away boy, might have thought and he doesn't
believe, is not a believer, doesn't seek to be pure, or righteous,
or mingled with forever, tasting it. He is simply crying and
unable, for heaven's sake, to cry any less or prevent small
howling bubbles of sound from escaping him and there is
no justification for his behaviour, he is not especially
mourning or damaged and this is exactly his problem, to be
frank, because he deserves no particular sympathy. All that
has happened is that time has passed and he isn't who he
was and never will be and occurrences have hurt him *tump
tump* and so he weeps and he would like a rest and so he
weeps and this boy, this man beseeches an intervention, but

has no faith in saviours and so he weeps and he knows he is commonplace and unrequited and so he weeps and he knows he is impossible and built around these small pieces, baffling pieces, ridiculous animal pieces, and so he weeps and he knows that he needs to be saved and he sings for it, tries to sing for it.

Everyone, he thinks, does try to sing for it.

His problem would be that he's making the wrong noise.

The Practice of Mercy

Dorothy used to dream in wonders, but that happened not so often now. Apart from the usual, there was no joy in pulling back a quilt and fitting herself snug to a sheet for that first touch of rest. She appreciated what was there: the cool cloth above and below and an inrush of what was gentle, was purely easing, but her nights remained unillustrated: sleep was simply fast, it seemed, and getting faster, no more than that. It would find her and immediately open itself in the manner of a soft but determined, familiar mouth. Yes, familiar was the word for it. Not miraculous.

Nevertheless, she had no real cause for complaint.

Insomnia would be worse.

Any number of things would be worse.

So she should take advantage of her current situation.

Dorothy's next stage in life, as many magazines and also human people told her, would involve increasingly extreme possibilities. Either she would be eaten by some irreversible dream and disappear, or else she would tackle older and older age – frayed bones, cascading dysfunctions – sustained by less and less unconsciousness. The old did not sleep, apparently. She would start to be up and about after three or two or fewer hours of respite from activity, outrunning the sun and desperate to knit, or bake, or to shout at lawn-digging squirrels until trespassing children dared her to summon up the deeper kinds of wrath. Leastways, these were the occupations of the elderly when Dorothy had been a long-dozing, shouted-at child. And there was sitting, of course. Sitting formed a tremendous focus for the waning and silvered, it once was their chief endeavour. It had been sort of heroic, the way old people sat. But as magazines and also human people told her, the current generation of over-sixties were mainly occupied with Internet shopping, exotic holidays, divorce and unprotected sex, perhaps in that order, perhaps not. This seemed a step forward, if not exactly up.

She wasn't sure she'd have the energy for all of that by then. Maybe not at the moment, either.

And low-income sexagenarians were probably sitting as usual, sitting as hard as ever, sitting and slumping and folding gradually towards the waiting horizontal, no sponsored sky-dives for them, no still-warm car keys chucked on the drawing-room table in hopes of a racy afternoon with widowers and widows.

Dorothy was taking a non-racy and non-exotic holiday. She'd needed a break and had made a point of letting sleep keep her late this initial morning, which meant that she'd missed whatever the hotel described as breakfast. This didn't upset her. She'd woken in enjoyably slow stages at the soft close of a somehow wearying night, showered and then eaten the banana left over from yesterday's travel before she stepped out for a potter in the town. A banana would do her fine until lunchtime. Tennis players and athletes in general ate them for potassium with positive effects at a cellular level.

She recalled a school chemistry lesson in which her teacher – Mr Collins, who sported an unfortunate type of ailing Chinese emperor's beard – had dropped a sliver of potassium into water. The whole class had then watched as the metal wasped back and forth on the liquid's surface in a tiny blur of lilac flames, too angry to sink. It made Dorothy smile, then and today: the idea that every human body hid a pastel shade of outrage no one should view without safety glasses, or else protective screens. It was a necessary element. Inside. The fuel for frenzy, beauty, frenzy, for evaporating types of heat was medically essential.

She breathed in sweetish, Middle Europeanish air – a sense of distant mountains about it and of overpriced market-place snacks closer at hand. The lane around her was either medieval, or a convincing reconstruction of bombed-flat houses, which had restored smoothed lintels, stooping doorways and colourful shutters, ornately impractical locks. What would once have been flammable and squalid accommodation, if not rubble heaps, had been turned into something charming – slightly too self-conscious and with ground floors mainly dedicated to the sale of alarming artisan ceramics, but cute. Relatively cute.

Dorothy padded along in her holiday shoes, feeling uncluttered and free from the need of garish mugs. Or lace, there was also lace. And contagious-looking biscuits. She believed it had been a good move on her part to avoid the dull, muzzy bustle around the hotel's buffet arrangements with morning strangers. She didn't like unknown quantities first thing – they were too much. Unsolicited early conversations made her tetchy as a maiden aunt facing down a squirrel.

Which was a good phrase. She must remember and say it for someone she knew. Although without a context it might fall flat.

Someone known was required for a good breakfast – either that, or solitude and culinary excitement. She'd liked the period a while ago when European breakfasts cut a mysterious dash with plates of unnameable meats and pure, wild colours of substances in jars and sealed little punnets of things that might be for on your foreign-looking bread, or for in the foreign-tasting coffee that would race beside your heart and rub it up into unnatural states, but you'd let it – far from home and a special occasion, you'd let it, you'd give the beats your leave to skip away on you.

These days, hotels practically everywhere had the same eggs, sausages, bacon, hash browns, French toast, the customary Anglo-American harbingers of obesity and doom. Dorothy continued to long for regional variations and mistakes – dishes of weird broth, unpardonable chicken sausages, potatoes to which sad accidents must have happened, strange grains and badly transfigured eggs. She sought out oddities whenever she could in order to encourage their continuance.

On her way back she would buy some of the worrying biscuits. She briefly wished her phrasebook included the question, 'Excuse me, do these taste bizarre, or have a disturbing texture, in which case I'll take several?'

Her banana had made for a bland, albeit nourishing, start and had not been – as it turned out – a quite adequate preparation for so much immaculate paintwork and so many small, deep windows full of burnished and horribly pointless ornaments. It all made her vaguely inclined towards vandalism or at least shouting and so she ducked off as quickly as she could to follow a footpath that dipped down a slope and abandoned the houses so it could cuddle the shade beside a stream. Eventually, the path thinned and become a chalky track. The mild breeze was grassy at this point, warm, and was flavoured with a sense of water, soaked leaves, secretive motion. Pheasants rose and battered up to the left of Dorothy, their tails straggling. As they laboured higher, they called out in stupid alarm: u-wa-u-wa-u-wa. Further on, they were less uneasy and merely let her drive them ahead, neatly trotting birds with the silhouettes of little fat men on horseback. Then they bustled off into undergrowth, rustles, nothing.

When the stream pooled and calmed under trees, she halted, relaxed.

There was an earthy and sandy bank, silent for footfalls and cool.

Dorothy had no precise idea which type of trees were stretched above her. Something in the style of birches.

She just stood.

It was clear there were fish in the pool, although she wasn't close enough to see, because a Labrador was wading about shin-deep and chasing them. The animal was avid: pouncing and stalking, tail wagging as it combed and quartered every hollow. Occasionally its belly dabbed down into what Dorothy guessed might be a pleasant chill. Beyond the damp and shadows, sunlight was sharpening overhead, already suggesting the need for reliefs.

Dorothy considered removing her shoes and paddling.

Perhaps once the dog had gone.

The animal seemed very busy, though, and jolly and disinclined to leave. As she watched, it snapped at the water, pressed its head full under and then shook itself free again, empty-mouthed, in a big startle of light that arced all round before landing in rings and sparks. Then it studied the wavelets again, entirely satisfied with the futility of its search. The pursuit was perfect, a twitchy and bright excitement. Finding, getting, that wasn't required.

Dorothy tried deciding – experimentally – that it wouldn't be a bad thing to wait here and see the dog being happy and have the shelter of dense-leaved, if unidentified, trees for a good while. Until dark, even. That could be a prudent choice.

Except then the dog's owner – she had to assume some kind of link between the two – began shouting what sounded like, 'Ankle, Ankle . . .' and came into view: middle-aged guy, wading along and naked except for faded and overly short denim shorts and with a balding ponytail, as if such a thing should be possible in a kind and proper world.

'Ankle! Ankle!' And, at this, the hunt stopped and there was a whiskery sneeze of delight and a paddling trot from the dog to bring it gladly beside its master. Then both glanced over at Dorothy, the man's expression implying that he – creepy, scraggle-armed and too undressed, his browned and hairy little stomach pouched shamefully over his waistband – he belonged in this place and was here every morning, and what the hell was she doing, intruding on the scene and peering at him and his beloved Ankle as if they were not quite right?

She didn't outstare him. She was aware, in fact, that

she'd started to blush and therefore had a kind of admission of guilt rising on her cheeks and neck, as if she'd intended to be here and to solicit bad interactions that ought to stay nameless. Like Ankle.

Who would call any pet Ankle?

The leaves sniggered hotly at her back as she withdrew, retraced her steps.

This left her alone with the path again and steering for town, because there was nowhere else aside from genuine hiking routes that led into the southern hills, for which maps were available from Reception. She didn't yet have a map, even though part of coming here had involved semi-plans for vigorous climbs and then worthwhile views accompanied by fruit, or bread and local sausage, regional cheese, decanted tap water from the metal bottle she'd packed with her boots and the largely superfluous compass intended to give her efforts an adventurous gloss. Every route was clearly and frequently signposted. There were inns every ten or twelve miles with rustic verandas and hygienic toilets. This was in no way a wilderness.

Possibly a wasteland. Probably. But not a wilderness.

In the pretty high street the pretty restaurants were crowded with lunching tourists. The tourists were not pretty, they were noisy and bewildering. Dorothy pressed open doors on clique after clique of happy tables, threaded herself under terrace parasols, found no comfortable space, found no space comfortable.

She wasn't hungry, anyway. That banana. Sustaining.

And the sunlight was making her head throb.

In the end, it turned out she could sit on the dark side of a repellent municipal statue, because no one else wanted to be there. Or because no one else was currently aware of its – she might term them – evasive charms. Others had been here, however: at the base of the thing, in under a mossy confusion of mythical tails and feet, was a shallow trough. Small-denomination coins lay calmly winking and shivering under its water, where they'd presumably been thrown: moderate, circular hopes or thanks for good luck, coming safely back, going safely home, finding contentment. She trailed her hand into the trough, made ripples and then stilled them. She lifted her fingers and licked them. They had no particular flavour: no hint of metal, no hint of luck. They were just colder than her lips.

She kept the imprint – index finger, second finger – in between her tongue and the roof of her mouth and let it be a reason for not speaking when she got up and searched again for an empty seat, found one, pointed to a laminated menu where it listed types of coffee, then sipped and paused and sipped and paused and then mimed – thumb snibbed against index finger in a tiny beak – the scribble of a bill.

She paid.

She scraped back her chair with a motion which seemed to her childish and liable to suggest that her limbs were uncivilised and out of scale. She felt it must surely be visible that she didn't share the range of interests and activities tucked up nicely inside the other visitors. She was trying to kill a day, make it go. Tomorrow she would have to try and kill another. It was making her feel brutal. It was worsening the headache.

Back at the hotel there would be, she was certain, no change and only another instalment of defeat.

She realised once more, kept realising, as if the information wouldn't stick, realised again how likely it was that someone you'd given the option of leaving, someone you'd said was free to go, that someone might not discover a way to come back. They might not have been looking for one, might always have intended the space that they've spent away should become permanent. It wasn't *away* for them any more – it was a different *here*. And someone might have got confused about who really left and what was lost and what broken and where the source of all the pain was; in absence, or presence, or alternative positions allowed to stay unexplored.

It was unclear.

And the streets were exhausted quickly, turned her constantly back to the unavoidable hotel.

A cool shower. A lie-down. Those wouldn't be bad things. She could appreciate them. If you operated at that level, it was relatively easy to be content.

Still, the foyer was slightly vicious in the way that it tumbled her up to the lift, hungry and amused, tilted her downhill so she couldn't help but rush to the room, to its door and the opening, the wide opening and the swing of revealed information: here was the wardrobe, here was the shuttered window and slivers of light, here was her case on the stand for cases, here was the bedside table, here was the bed.

Here was a different here and a different bed.

Here was the bed.

Here was her headache slowing, relenting so unexpectedly that it made her close to tearful.

Here was the chair with shoes beneath it, neat, and a more untidy slump of clothes: shirt, jeans, underpants, socks, the glimmer of a metal wristwatch also removed.

Here was the bed.

Here was the relenting bed.

'I got tired.'

'Yeah?'

'Yeah.'

Here was the space around the bed, a little uncrossable and surprised.

'Where were you?'

'Where were you?'

Here was the bed where he was sitting up at the sound of her, sitting up like Sunday morning, sitting up like ages and ages ago when it made her smile. He had the covers tucked under his arms and he did not look as if he'd been sleeping, or resting since he arrived. He looked as if he'd decided the weight of talking to her would be eased if he was undressed, but now he was reconsidering.

Dorothy frowned and then stopped, because otherwise she would appear to be unhelpful. 'I was in the town – village.' She went to sit on the bed, but then didn't. Since it was, to a degree, altered, she had no longer been there before and was nervous of it.

'I did call when they told us the flight was . . . I knew you'd have your phone off.'

'I had my phone off.'

'I know.'

They both understood that uncomfortable calls she has to answer make her turn off her phone pre-emptively. It was irritating. Neither of them would have denied that.

'So I landed in this . . . I'd forgotten how much I like it here. It was a good idea. Good idea. And thanks for letting me know. We can have some days. Really. Clever. I wouldn't have thought . . . but you did . . .' He lay down flat and blinked at the ceiling as if he were an invalid, an injured party, a boy overcome by his surroundings. 'I had to catch a train . . . They landed us in the wrong place. Then a train.' He disappeared his arms under the quilt and tucked it neat to his chin from inside, from in the dark and hiding. 'A train . . .' It was too hot to be so covered.

Dorothy turned, sat on the floor with the back of her head leaned against the mattress, against the modest shifts of motion that told her he was there. She told him, 'I wish I hadn't . . . I wish I . . .'

'I didn't want you to think that I wasn't coming. I was going to. The pause wasn't about that.'

She didn't tell him anything.

'You worry. You get anxious.'

She didn't tell him anything.

'And I get . . .'

She didn't tell him anything.

'I worry, too . . . You've seen and . . . I'm . . . I wanted you to know I was on my way.'

There was a small ruffle of bed sounds and he reached down and pressed her shoulder and the back of his hand was brushed untidily against her cheek and then he formed the touch again and moved through it again and concentrated and she could feel his purpose as tender, serious, frightened.

They had broken things, the pair of them. Unexpected damage had occurred, and they'd thought they would have managed better after their years of practice, but they hadn't.

She leaned into his hand, kissed his fingers. 'I got scared.'

'I know.' She heard him breathe out and pictured a column

of something, some living trouble, pluming above his face. 'And when you . . . That was . . . I don't think . . .'

This at the moment was peaceful. No breakages.

'I wanted to hear your voice.'

'I'm sorry.'

And there is a way of saying this which means *we can't continue* and a way of saying it which means *we can keep on and manage and we can be all right.*

'I'm sorry. I'm sorry, too.'

Knocked

His earliest adult experience – he wakes up in a hospital wearing stiff clothes, cold clothes. Also there is a some kind of mistake in his head. He is not alarmed, the boy, only puzzles in the cloth- and sour-tasting darkness of the ward until he knows it *is* a ward and that something has gone wrong and put him here.

'Nurse?'

The boy does not say this. He would never have thought to call a nurse: his character is undemanding and, besides, he cannot imagine needing anything beyond perhaps an explanation for the maritime rush which is catching at his ears and this dizzy, laden weakness of his thinking.

'Nurse?'

It is this word that woke him, he believes – its repetition. First word of his alternate life.

'Nurse?'

Footfalls consent to be summoned and close on him, as fast as irritation – heel-thumps before toe-thumps and a squeak each time they argue with the floor.

The nurse's shape halts three beds down from the boy

and interrupts the glimmers of a window in a way that seems peculiarly shocking.

'What do you want, then?'

She is nothing like the boy's mother, has a voice which is entirely strange to him, and sharpened – it sews through the air, passes over him, then on. He hears it ting against the farthest wall.

'Well?'

'Can I have a glass of water?' The melody of the question is indecisive, apologetic.

'No.'

And the nurse-shape begins to leave again, even more quickly, while the boy wonders if the other child, the thirsty one – who sounds like a boy, too – will maybe die soon from a lack of water. Water does seem such a plain and reasonable requirement that only some fatal intention would allow it to be denied.

Lying still and heavier than he has ever been, the boy recoils very slightly within his unfamiliar pyjamas. He believes, almost at once, that these are part of the belongings of some previous small patient who has died while on the ward, odds and ends reused for the benefit of others and no further trace remaining. There are numerous, uncountably numerous, places where the boy's skin is being touched by the dead-boy cloth. The jacket cuffs nuzzle clammily against his wrists. It is very likely his arse is where a dead-boy's arse has been, and moreover his parts which are meant to be secret are comfortably settled in these trousers, perhaps because this is how the dead-boy's used to rest. His mickey where another mickey was. A smoky rush seems to rummage across him as he considers this and his left hand sneaks beneath the covers to make sure of himself and feel that all is well.

The hand seems slower and more clever than it used to be.

'Nurse?' The boy tries his own mouth with the word and it emerges much as he'd expected.

'Yes.' She has paused because he has spoken and this makes him proud, but wary of coming responsibilities. 'Yes, what do you want?'

'Can I have a glass of water?' He isn't thirsty, only curious.

'Yes.'

And the water is brought to him, shining with guilt, and set between his palms when he has raised himself through a wavering and thickened space. The boy holds his drink with monumental care – has to concentrate on gripping, as if he might soon forget how. He clings to the smoothness of the glass, to someone else's want, sips and swallows loudly and with a kind of grin.

'Why does my head hurt?' Because it does – the left side of his skull and even his cheek are singing with a weird, dark awareness, something exhilarating.

'A horse trod on you.'

This seems not unlikely.

He tucks the water inside himself, understands it is coiled now in a blue shape that perhaps half-fills him. 'Thank you.' He is polite. His father and mother would expect that of him. Then he slides back down to be flat, the water lapping and giggling as he moves.

A horse.

Yes.

There were horses.

There were lessons with horses to make the boy confident and able to sit up straight, a commanding presence in later life. A premeditated Christmas present which had started in January: ten o'clock on Saturday mornings, an hour with himself and various older, wilier boys in a wide, high barn – peaty and sawdusty stuff underfoot and everywhere alive with a humid and dangerous reek. Frost beyond the walls, but the boy hot, the boy feverish with horses.

They were large in the manner of trees – a threat of falling about them, of terrible damages waiting in the hollow-sounding jaws and the long bones of their faces, the fierce, unsettled gouging of their hooves. They were big machinery with sudden blares of unpredictable intention, eyes that could not be relied upon. Hoisted and struggled up on to the leather-creak and sway of their backs, the boy was too astonished to recall what he ought to do with his hands, his heels, his spine, his legs, his courage and his common sense. These were things that he could not cling to, that he lost in the massive breathing of every animal.

At eleven-fifteen on Saturday mornings he would sit in the back of his parents' car, being taken home, and he would smell of animals and improperly hidden fear. He would experimentally consider that his pain tomorrow – there always was pain the day after – might be easier if he had been beaten, that his bruises would be less shaming then.

No one has, in fact, beaten the boy at any time – although his mother did once hit him hard across the face and he does not know why. His father was already crying when this happened and the boy believes the crying was ready and prepared for him, his jolted mouth, the idea that he might be knocked into sense, into being a proper and undisappointing boy. The incident made him feel briefly and overly close to both his parents. Of course, he has often read stories where English boys are *flogged* in vast and incomprehensible schools and there are no parents – he sees it as wicked that he treasures these scenarios, prefers them to his current reality.

The boy holds thoughts he cannot name, he hates and wants and wants and hates his endless failures and the yelling instructor in the barn and the better riders' indolent disgust. On the drives home his parts which are meant to be secret will occasionally flinch and tease and he will form blurred wishes to be simplified, destroyed and built up better again from nowhere.

When his mother and father ask him if he enjoys his riding lessons, he tells them, 'Yes.'

Although today – yesterday – the boy is pleasantly unsure of when – he was saved from having to tell his parents anything.

This is how you get to be alone in hospital.

A horse.

It was called Crombie and was yellowish and had a famously bad temper. It had known he was afraid.

That morning they were strung and circled outside in a field – no more barn, because this was meant to be the spring – March – but the ground was stiff again, ice layers cracking over empty ruts and slush where the sunlight was lying. Crombie didn't like the cold. Crombie strayed and head-shook and his beast-mind turned, the boy could taste it, towards racing and hurts. The boy was in a slithery panic before the horse's hooves ever dug in hard, or the charge ever started, the bolt.

No one had told the boy how to stop a bolting horse.

Some shouting, somebody loomed alongside him, reaching for the reins, but this drove Crombie faster and out on to tarmac, out to a road, out into a blind-white pitching sky, lashing breath, gripping, sweating and the small decision, and then much larger, that the boy should let go, must be over with this and drop.

Head injury.

In what is still the boy's favourite legend a man fell from a ladder and was given a head injury, and when he woke he could see to the future and find whatever anybody needed.

This made him famous.

He was called Peter.

Which is the boy's name.

Head injury.

The man was Dutch – being from Holland means you're Dutch.

Which is confusing.

Dutch sounds like Scotch, but Scotch is a drink and Scottish is a person, so the boy is not Scotch – the boy's mother and father are quite sure about that. They are thoroughly Scottish in every way.

If he says he is Scotch he will be wrong.

If he laughs too out-loud he will be wrong.

If he spoons his soup towards himself he will be wrong.

It would be equally wrong for the boy to keep a hard want burning at his heart, a need to draw in calamity and knocks.

He does it anyway.

And now he has a *head injury* of his own. He holds it like a smile poured in under his hair.

The boy pictures his brain as newly alert and changed to a glistening mass, a larger cousin of the oyster his grandfather made him eat last summer – told him it was living, that it would forage and thrive beneath his skin and scour him out into a better health. He is sure the accident has roused his oyster-mind and that it is currently flexing, searching forward with an appetite he admires. He hopes it has decided to look for his future, to bring it back and show him the ways it could be.

The boy is not alarmed when some kind of effort, some kind of striving, presses his eyelids unstoppably shut and sets the night running and swinging and plunging him to sleep. He leaves himself and travels.

He remembers – dreams and remembers – the other time he saw his father cry. His daddy had been singing: head back and the words there, red and wet in the mouth and, at the end of them, a weeping.

The boy's manhood and contentment, he feels, will be built in evenings when he is grown and sings, and there are men about him and hugs which cuff his skull and magnificent griefs, such marvellous injuries to shape him and let him rage. These will be hurts he can be proud of, historic and honourable.

Then he pictures his mother's table, her dining-room table on which he must not ever lean his elbows during meals. It shines oddly, ripples and draws his attention to stand beside it and peer down. Laid out along the mahogany he sees his older body, naked and washed. The boy studies his wish to be solid, short-bearded, complete, and to have impressive arms with one tattoo – a little flag with writing underneath it, which he cannot read, but realises is important. His parts which are meant to be secret remain as he knows them – *a little boy's mickey, always* – and then fade – *goodbye mickey*. Somehow, he spills away.

It seems a proper punishment that when his parts are gone they haunt him more than ever. They sting.

And the boy then sees himself opened like a book while hands dig out the truth of him, work wrist-deep, and find a rifle and a chanter, the shine of a plough, forgetfulness twice-distilled, broom flowers and roses, a lobster upended and balanced on its claws, a woman's hair dragged from its scalp and thick as jute, a righteous and clever tawse, a burning rivet and a burning brand and a burning cross and a burning word, a collar the colour of blood, a whale bone carved with a ship and on the ship a man who travels, who will scour the world, burn it, bleed it, thieve it out and suffer as he steps, heavy and mad as horses, and held in his hand is a heart, a sleeping heart, a hunted heart, a slave heart, a heart like a hole through to nowhere that he lifts above his head.

He waves to the boy and the boy waves back.

This waving troubles the boy – it shivers him and makes him rock.

'Hold still.'

He is seasick as he rises up into the ward, turns conscious, hears the tiny panting of the pressure cuff as it inflates. His arm is throbbing and troubles him.

'I said hold still. You can do that, can't you?' The nurse, another nurse, whispering. 'You're a big boy. Can't you do what you're told?'

This will be a predictable element of his recovery. Every three hours, night and day, someone will come to measure the condition of his blood, put the chill of a thermometer under his tongue.

'Don't bite it.'

For the boy this will be wearying and unheroic.

Tomorrow afternoon his mother will arrive and sit next to his bed with a new copy of *The Beano* and *The Dandy* and, in a paper bag, the *Oor Wullie* annual he was not allowed for Christmas, because it is full of rough talk and ways in which nobody decent should behave. His father will not visit, but will sit in the parked car outside and listen to football reports on the radio – this will be because the smell of hospitals makes him sick. He will send his best. If he knew about the *Oor Wullie* annual then he would not.

The boy will take his comics and his mother's kiss on his forehead and on the one of his cheeks that is nearest to her. He will think he doesn't want to read, because he suspects reading might be difficult, but he won't say that, for fear of being rude. He will not know what to do when he sees that she is very sad about him, and so he will pretend that his head hurts more than it does and she will nod a lot and put a bottle of Lucozade wrapped in crinkling yellow stuff on the bedside cabinet which is his while he is here and then she will stand up and he will suddenly regret that she is leaving.

Once he is alone he will still have the scent of her against his skin. And he will catch the only true hint he'll ever get from his future – that there will be times when that exact perfume strikes him, makes him open like a book and ask to be hurt by strangers until he cannot think. This doesn't unsettle him, is merely strange. He assumes it is the first of many insights and, sitting up in bed – little boy, little mickey

– he is happy. The crack to his skull has left him brilliant with wishes, unsteadied by apparently too many opening paths towards glories. He has been thoroughly punished in advance and this means that his powers will be remarkable.

All the Rage

Mark had never thought he'd consider throwing himself under a train. Turned out he was wrong. *Not for the first time.*

Cheap shot, I realise, but I always do take the cheap shot. I wouldn't really be me without it.

But I am me and I have been – with assistance – very badly wrong. Repeatedly.

At least the weather was okay. Hot, in fact: the light bleaching and withering down at everyone while they waited on a platform which wasn't their platform at a station they shouldn't have reached. This was not on the way to anywhere anybody had meant to be and apparently no services ever stopped here. It didn't even seem to be a place for people, rather for goods, repairs in sidings, arcane mechanical processes. Mark could smell ageing oil and traces of coal dust. There was a sense beyond that of gap sites, bomb sites, failed reconstructions after the war.

The last world war, not the current succession of little wash-and-goes.

He found himself reminded of his childhood, the shoddy old home town and his lovingly rehearsed escapes therefrom.

And he had escaped, of course, quite quickly. Clever youngsters still could then and he was clever: full grant to go and play at studying in a mediocre, but blessedly far-removed university. He didn't look back.

And as for going back, turning up again – nobody would have thanked me for trying that. Best to do all concerned the big, merciful favour and disappear.

He now had a presentable London postcode, loft extension, Polish au pair with a marine-biology degree – or zoology, something like that – and the ability to amplify his griefs at the hands of a rail network in crisis by writing about them – *yet more suffering imposed on blameless middle classes* – for a national daily paper. But none of his life's securities meant that he wasn't still ready to doubt the station signs. His current home and circumstances felt immediately unconvincing when he got stressed. There'd be this creep of ridiculous suspicion: maybe he wasn't where he thought, maybe over the bridge would be that other, original shithole and his place in it waiting for him, irrevocable. He'd spin on his heel and here would be Mum in the loud-walled sitting room catching a breather before tea, hands worried nonetheless with knitting, or sewing, or Christ knew what – and odd, sweet ham for sandwiches, stuff you got out of a tin – and his dad back from the garage – and smoking on buses and trains, and ciggies being advertised on telly – ciggies everywhere – and cheap pullovers that sparked up blue with static when you peeled them off fast in the dark. You'd never get girls with a pullover like that.

Not with a pullover at all. Not to a satisfactory degree.

He was out, though, truly long gone and free and he hadn't even once been forced, for professional reasons, to offer deferential and trustworthy smiles to strangers with broken cars and he didn't need a girl, he had a wife.

I'm just stuck here at the moment, where nothing stops. It really does – nothing stays here and you have to breathe it in. I am inhaling the stink of nothing.

His imagination bridled before it could fully recall the scent of his own skin on Sunday mornings: shifting the covers and catching that mustiness, tiredness. He smelled of nothing. It was on him.

A long lie and a touch of sweat and Pauline already virtuously about in the garden, or the kitchen, or her church.

I always do think of it as her personal church, because she does, and who am I to disagree?

But there he would be, stagnant and upstairs and holding on around an hour, or maybe two, of peace.

Mark was very fond of peace. Increasingly.

Pauline was less inclined towards the tranquil.

Mercurial. Why I married her. I'm sure. At least partly that.

That and she thought she was pregnant. Turned out she was wrong. It's a trait we share, our fondness for the wrong.

But I did also love the way she could kick off and stay off, generate these heartfelt torrents of fury. She has retained the capacity to be magnificent in that area and I continue to admire it.

I truly do.

It was plain that she wanted a row at the moment, was quietly and almost sexily brooding on the words she might say, were she not surrounded by a mass of other non-travelling travellers. She'd ask him again – rhetorical question – why he couldn't have driven them over from London and right to the arse-end of Wales for no very good reason, other than to let her see her friends. She got this urge, once a year or so, to wear spotless wellingtons and padded faux-country coats with her friends, to drink red wine until it stained her mouth to an injury, also with her friends, to exert a vague authority over a herd of pye-dog children – long-haired and ill-mannered and airily illiterate – with her continual bloody friends who had produced said children without considering that parenthood would mean being broke and staying in the arse-end of Wales, while acting as if it was Italy and wandering hunch-backed streets in a migraine of drizzle.

He couldn't have driven. It would have made him tired. Correction, it would have made him exhausted – there and back would have made him dead. This last week had wiped him out. He'd been a wreck by Wednesday, Kempson ranting and condemning them to additional white nights, threatening more redundancies while they sorted out urgent copy to go with urgent tits.

This week's tits were wronged and glazed with anguish, always a favourite. They were classy tits, married to a Special Adviser tits, the prime minister's full confidence still placed in their husband tits, late of Cheltenham Ladies' College and rumours of early spliffs and precocious rapacities tits. They'd probably got an opinion on Gypsies, too. Or tax-avoidance. Austerity. The future of the euro. Frankly tragic that they had no power of speech. Infinitely disappointing that their owner did.

Christ!

So no stamina left for long-haul chauffeuring.

Sorry.

Sorry that you had your precious break, but now its

even more precious afterglow has been destroyed by my boorish insistence on not having a heart attack.

So very sorry indeed.

An apology should have been unnecessary in a friendly world, but was offered in any case. The world wasn't friendly.

Sorrysorrysorrysorry.

The usual rolling hiss. The sound of my head: like a detuned radio, or the drag of an old-time needle over old-time vinyl at the end of the record, once the music's stopped.

Pauline should have known better than to ask. She was fully aware of Mark's persistent, historic aversion to motor vehicles.

Grew up with five petrol-head brothers, didn't I?

What sensible parent has that many kids? That many sons? That many of anything?

Mark had been the late and tender afterthought, putting an end to the line. No more soft-pawed fighting and solemnly blue jokes to share with Dad as if they were presents from an oncoming life.

Don't tell your mother, and having a laugh and sipping from a fag round the back, leaned against the wall – all the Burroughs boys together.

He'd pretty much ruined things, because from the outset Mark had been a poor fit with his father and the boys. He'd known that he made them uncomfortable: kind, but stilted and uneasy.

I didn't like what they liked.

While his siblings couldn't wait to get dirty, he had always hated engines, tinkering, manual tasks of every kind. He would, as an adult, abandon some type of large Renault because it was actually on fire. Not overheating, but wildly ablaze due to unforgivable negligence on his part. He'd left it in a lay-by, run away.

Wasn't even my car. Borrowed. And not returned.

If she'd known about this – it was before her time – he could imagine how Pauline would react, pronouncing the three syllables of *typical* as only she could. She needn't be furious to make the word ring like a curse. Authentically injurious.

For now, she whipped a glance at him, gave it some strength. Mark was aware that the tall bloke in retro corduroy, or just very misguided corduroy, had read their little exchange – Pauline's threat, Mark's obeisance – and was smiling in response.

But you're wrong, chum. My relationship is not the nightmare you assume. You have no reason to feel you are lucky and can be smug. You don't understand.

There was something about kissing her while she tasted of contempt – there was a depth in that, an intoxication. You had to be careful in these areas and he wouldn't recommend it for someone who flagged under tension, but if you could stand it . . .

Wasted on him, the corduroy man. Moron.

Mark shifted in an intentionally obvious way to eye the moron's female companion, give her some time. She was unimpressive.

'Mark.'

Bite the tongue and don't say 'Yes, dear.' It's such a cliché.

'Yes, darling.'

'Go and find something out.'

'Of course. I'll go and find something out.'

And Mark did indeed step lively, as if he were seeking more up-to-date information and could be ordered about and relish it. The crowd was hungry for distraction and a theatrically craven husband drew attention. He could feel the pity and amusement lap towards him as he trotted on, a tide of nasty satisfaction.

Stare if you want. Take a picture, I don't mind. I still know what you don't – that there are opportunities for a mature and fulfilled enjoyment in my situation.

He switched through to the other platform, the one in shade. It was deserted and his body lifted, was stroked by being out of sight.

I'll give it ten minutes, have my own precious break.

There was no reason to do more: at mysterious intervals a man came and, in a perversely quiet voice, told the crowd of would-be passengers that their train would arrive in twenty minutes. He had done this several times in the last three hours. Should Mark be able to locate him, the man would doubtless repeat the twenty-minute claim, because this was precise and therefore not frustrating and seemed to promise a not unreasonable wait.

The electronic indicator board sometimes showed their train and sometimes others, none of which appeared. Mark had decided he'd take the rest of the day in soft focus and so wasn't wearing his glasses. This meant the shiny, tiny letters and fictional times simply flared together into uncommunicative blocks. He preferred them like that.

In his absence, Pauline could consult the board. She had her glasses.

Doesn't like them, because she's decided they make her look old.

They make her look like her mother, which isn't old.
It is much worse than old.

And meanwhile they weren't without the useless kind of trains, non-stopping anonymous trains: long, high blurs of weight and violence that gashed the air and ravaged past, leaving him breathless and tempted.

Suicide as an alternative to marriage.
Well, I wouldn't put it that bluntly.
No.
But there is a tug as they roar on by, the illusion of longing.

A voice from who knew where – it was a woman's – would give them notice through the PA system before the tearing intrusion of each express, but nevertheless he couldn't quite prepare enough. They made him feel undefended, almost naked.

If you stand too near the edge you'll be drawn off by sheer velocity and crushed. I read that somewhere.

The trains were so plainly unsurvivable and disinterested. They were attractive. Marvellous.

The impact of another troubled the fabric of everything briefly and he wished he'd been closer for it, over with Pauline. She wouldn't have stood too near. She was, in fact, probably sitting as he'd left her with knees tight together and ankles tucked into one side as a lady should. Their case was taking her weight.

It has a hard shell.

Inside it, their belongings didn't mix – his shirts and underpants in a tangle, Pauline's laundry compressed into subsidiary containments. They had separate sponge bags, too.

Got to keep those toothbrushes apart.

There was no café for him to visit and find her placating treats. The whole trail of those evicted from the previous, ailing train had been ushered along barren walkways, down steps and far from the station proper, which had been mean and small enough in itself. Not even a vending machine. No apparent staff. Mark couldn't imagine where the twenty-minute man could be keeping himself before he emerged to murmur about fake arrivals and departures.

Mark drifted until he was standing in one of the broad alleys that led back to the crowds, the platform, the wait. He was quite a distance from Pauline and safely unobservable.

Probably.

He glanced through to the phoning and pacing of his fellow castaways. The bustle was thin at this point.

But you're there, aren't you? By yourself. That's you.

He'd noticed the woman earlier, taken note.

And I'm looking at you.

She was in her late forties and her spine had settled into something of a slump, but she had an optimistic wardrobe. There were flowers, lots of flowers: a light skirt, thin blouse, mildly bohemian, hoping to conceal that she was fatter than she'd like. Mark knew it would be a safe bet that she'd have a messy flat and would sneak bits of food in the kitchen before she came out to eat properly with a guest. Flat shoes, but good calves. Goodish curves. Accustomed to being unappreciated.

But you have my undivided attention.

And if he thought it louder.

You have my undivided attention.

Sure enough, she turned, tugged by his awareness, and

he did what he wasn't allowed to do – no longer wanted to do, if he was truthful – and faced the woman and was nothing for her.

That's you. By yourself. And this is me. By myself. And I'm nothing.

I am very much nothing: not serious, not long-term, neither heartfelt, nor heart-breaking, not intrusive, not a burden, not anyone who'll ever know you and therefore be irritated or repelled.

I will be good and easy and meaningless.

Mark smiled.

I'm nothing.

He considered himself.

And I have a nice arse.

I have an excellent arse. Frequently complimented.

Early forties – forty-four is early forties – but thirty-nine to look at and with more-than-satisfactory legs. They give me the height, the perspective. One could say they lead the eye. Up. And I'm keeping my hair well, dark and thick.

Plus, I have kind eyes.

And no glasses, which means that I'm currently loosening her edges, Vaselining over my appreciation of someone who would benefit from blurring.

Late forties for a woman is catastrophic. She has my sympathy.

And this me, this nothing – she could have that, too.

He ambled forward to lean in the last shade of the passage, on the blind side from his wife.

You could have it all and it's a lot, it's really something.

He smiled again, folded his arms.

My arms around myself, because you have not held me and yet I do need to be held. It's such a shame for both of us.

And the woman smiled.

That's right. You're made for nothing, you are – made for it.

She kept him in view when he moved and then as he halted.

And he knew absolutely that he should be business-like here, should claim her, because she would love it. Because how unlikely and beautiful it would be for anyone – but perhaps particularly for her – that a stranger should be jerked to a stop by who you are and then swiftly driven to helpless and expert improprieties.

Every one of the possible acts was prohibited, but he did rush harmlessly through thoughts of how thin the woman's bra and blouse were and how they would give her away once he'd talked her horny.

Private tits, quiet tits, tits that will never be shown to a jaded nation.

But she'd show me.

She wouldn't want it stated. Our conversation would be pleasantly oblique. We'd talk about this journey, other journeys, other passengers, anything really, it wouldn't matter as long as I kept the music of it rubbing forward and no chance for her to doubt. I needn't say anything filthy, just keep a hunger in the smiles, the right catch in the eyes, and by the time our train came I'd get her on board and then have her in a toilet.

Done it before.

She wouldn't realise it had been sordid until tomorrow,

maybe the end of the week. Today it would be passion and romance.

And then tidy up and out into the carriage. I'd suggest that we sit apart afterwards, because of what fun that would be: acting like she'd never met me, when I'm still a ghost between her legs.

Those red plush silk and shaky minutes between her legs.

I could tell her if she's good that we'd do it again past Swindon.

Maybe not a lie.

Maybe give her my genuine number and save hers. Hook up, if we felt like taking longer and she didn't live ridiculously far away.

Although there is much to be said for women who live ridiculously far away and the trend towards exponential fare increases for public transport. And petrol's hardly a bargain.

We could improvise.

She would let me.

Sometimes people want nothing. It is a necessity.

But then Mark gave her an altered smile.

And this is to say that I would if I could.

And it is such a pity I can't.

Have this instead – the sting of possibility. It's a much neater present, a nice one: the way that your body will rouse and insist where I would have kissed it.

You know the places. You do.

Mark let his hands fall sadly and, because he considered this polite, he whispered his knuckles against the woman's as he passed her, headed into the glare and walked to offer Pauline interwoven lies.

'Well, you won't believe it, but they said another twenty minutes.'

I really did go and speak to someone and serve you as you wished.

'Sorry, darling. It's outrageous.'

I am not 40 or 50 per cent turned on.

'I could go back. If you want, love.'

I wouldn't like to scream until it hurts me.

'But I don't think it would be much use, and the sun's giving me a headache. I feel a bit out of it, actually . . .'

I am not thumbing through random memories of working inside other women until I felt the sweat run, the insect tickle of being entirely waylaid.

'I am sorry.' And he kissed her, squeezed her hand in his.

She withdrew from the pressure and pursed her lips. Mark took pains to understand her point of view.

That's sixteen years of history between us in one motion – and having no kids and her needing her glasses more badly than I need mine. Varifocals.

That's me having, thus far, decided not to be dead yet and this causing a further difference of opinion.

Their history wasn't uniformly bleak. Nobody's ever was, not without significant rewriting. For three years he'd been relatively happy and as faithful to Pauline as a rescued dog. Then he had rather reverted to type and it was hugely regrettable and he did feel bad about it, but equally he'd never let her know. He hadn't insisted they share an open marriage and hadn't been prone to regular confessions. He hadn't confessed at all.

Because I was nothing. So I had nothing to confess.

I *washed thoroughly after them, extra soap and water for the hands, the betraying hands, and I used mouthwash and set aside a holdall of specifically adulterous clothing – like a gym bag. Salted money away for the costs. I suppressed my traces.*

She didn't know.

Not a clue about the girl I met in a hotel car park during a late-night fire alarm, the girl on an overnight train to Berlin, a woman who'd slept with Mick Jagger – him or Keith, definitely one of the Stones: being with her was like trying on a vintage coat – and a woman who'd been crying at a party, a conference waitress, multiple attendees of multiple conferences, the wife of a friend – which was stupidly risky – the wives of strangers, the assistant in a chemist's shop after hours. During hours would have been silly.

The pin from her name badge scratched my cheek.

It was a little bit relentless.

But consistent – all nothing.

Then he'd woken on a Sunday early, been dressed and spruce at breakfast, as if he'd had an appointment. Indeed, he'd taken advantage of the day's suggested shape and tone – it seemed spruce and forthright, somehow – and had claimed – why not – that he was suddenly needed at the office and would nip out while Pauline set forth to tend the weeds.

Plants – she tends the plants.

She kills the weeds.

As far as I'm aware, she does it that way round.

I told her a chef – controversial, but adored by female readers – had forgotten to tell us that he was dyslexic/thick/

on a bender – I wasn't listening at the time so I'm unsure of my final choice – and would fail to provide 900 pithy words about something or other I couldn't recall. I didn't think it related to cooking. Probably he was attempting to reposition his persona. Pauline is fascinated by B-List hubris and so this entertained her.

I said it was best to show my face, go in and deal with the minor disaster, catch up on my expenses – they're more like begging letters now – and be the chap on hand for any further emergencies. We lived in straitened times, even then, and I needed to seem flexible and willing.

I also did honestly want some fresh air.

No, I didn't.

I wanted to keep an appointment I hadn't made.

He'd caught the Tube.

Piccadilly Line: convenient and it's my favourite shade of blue.

He'd stepped into an empty carriage.

And she followed.

That was you.

That was you, Emily.

That was you.

She'd sat opposite, a tiny clumsiness in her movements that lit him, put him on alert, even though she'd been unremarkable in many ways.

Sweet Jesus, that was you.

An over-large biker jacket had made her seem round-shouldered.

As if she was shy about having breasts.

Emily.

That was sweet and you.

Her costume fought ungracefully to combine revelation with concealment. She'd made a series of unimaginative and self-punishing choices in red and mainly black: holed black tights and layers of equally wounded T-shirts, short denim shorts and high-lacing boots with industrial soles. One hand was curled intently round a can of cider.

Didn't know your name, but that was sweet and you.

Mark had watched her face, its flickers and hints as it flirted with insecurity, or gave him little signs of pride – the happy and personal victory that was her cider, the wish to be challenging.

Lowered eyes and faking that I wasn't there for you, but I already was. Immediately.

And then she made a small retreat into hurts, or the threat of hurts, their memory, and into some variety of fear. He'd shivered with a vast and irrational compulsion to disclose and remove every wound for her.

Sweet you.

Now and then she had the expression of someone preserved in an untouched space, of dispassionate observation. Her skin was pale as paper and not especially clean and clearly the cider was there to help her up out of the night before, to remove a disreputable pain, but there was so, so much strange purity there, too. He would come to define this sanctity and distance as her principal characteristics. That morning they simply caught him, along with the rest. She was twenty-two – not genuinely young – but the grace of childhood hadn't faded on her.

Like all the proper ones – the real alcoholics, before they blow – she had this weird perfection, was flawless because of her flaws and made them a beauty.

She was angelic.

Stupid word.

My angel.

Shining with each of the obvious violations.

She was self-inflicted.

He had known how catastrophic she would be, a coma patient could have realised that Emily was dangerous. He hadn't been deterred.

Quite the reverse.

The first thing she'd said to him was 'Perv'. But she'd made it sound affectionate – warm and for him in the empty carriage – and they'd stayed where they were, discarded any prior plans and ridden out to the terminals at Heathrow – not particularly speaking, only being with each other, rocking onwards inside the shudders of the carriage. The seats around them gently silted up with voyagers and their unwieldy bags and then mostly emptied as people Mark felt were entirely unnecessary left for exciting, or happy, or business-related destinations. By Turnham Green she'd come to him, switched places and sat at his side.

On their way back into town – the line had returned them, as if it approved of Mark's intentions – he'd taken her hand, completely unsure of whether she'd consent. He hadn't a clue how to play her.

She stole my game.

But by Covent Garden he'd risked standing and leading her out and away through the station and up to the fast-breathing world.

There I was with Emily and the sky not the same as it had been and the structure of myself softly altering and rampaging.

He'd found them a fairly quiet bar where he drank cider with her – he detested cider – so their mouths would taste the same.

I knew wherever she lived would be appalling and indiscreet, so I picked her a hotel.

Without bags, unwieldy or otherwise, I got to enjoy an amount of lying at the check-in desk. They sold me a pair of toothbrushes to replace the ones we hadn't lost in a spurious suitcase that hadn't been misdirected to Tenerife. I held both the brushes together in one hand, made sure they touched as we strolled to the lift.

All concerned were under no illusions about what we were going to do.

She didn't seem to mind and didn't seem not to.

Three weeks after my fortieth birthday and I got myself a twenty-two-year-old.

Or she got me.

Beyond the fantasy luggage, I didn't lie about anything else when I was with her. I made it a rule from then on. I told her about Pauline. I told her I'd have to leave way before the morning. I told her about my habits. I told her about me.

It was a first.

Nothing changed.

Nothing was absolutely changed.

Almost immediately, his enthusiasm for the others dissipated. He had a handful of repeat offenders, but he simply didn't ring them any more and, as a consequence, they drifted. He'd been a man who was mainly attracted to passing trade and he let it pass.

He had Emily.

It was a devotion of sorts.

There were slippery, sick days when she didn't answer his calls. She never explained why. He decided to assume the problem was related to technical issues and bought her a new phone. It was pink, which made it a joke, but he also meant it very much and didn't want her to lose it – hence the ghastly colour. Before he handed it over, he'd stood in the shop and nestled the thing beside his cheek.

Hello. You'll be here and my voice in your hands.

But mainly she was quite reliable and willing to meet him at various hotels near Euston, or King's Cross – his choice – suitably anonymous and seedy establishments.

Perhaps the only thing that limited how often they could be together was his ability to hide the cost of this or that dog-eared double room.

Perhaps he believed he would be lost if he saw her too frequently.

Because she was wholly willing. She gave him the purgatory of that.

Her acceptance – unrelenting acceptance – put a terror in his blood, a type of recurring vertigo. Whatever he requested, she would do: she would dress as he dictated, with barely a hesitation. She would be naked – he was very predictable – beneath her coat and visit bars with him in Loughborough Junction, Ealing, Hampton, places where he wouldn't be known.

Hand slipped between her buttons in a cab coming back from Croydon and what I found, what I found, the deep sweet, my best girl's ache.

Laughing in another hotel lift, on the rise, not being what you'd call subtle.

He explored her with harsh appetites for which he blamed her and also thanked her and also blamed her, helplessly punishing and offering. He possessed each access to her, tired her and she allowed him. He tied her up and took advantage, bought a dedicated camera for recording the indignities and marvels, her splendours.

For several months he stripped and beat her on each of their nights and she made no objection, made no sound. He didn't intend to hurt her, but spanking was insufficient, so the shameful slap of his belt carried, no doubt, into neighbouring rooms, as did his own cries, his attempts to destroy her silence.

Which was the last straw.

In the end, her acquiescence broke his ingenuity.

Emily made a new nothing. She made it permanent.

He didn't want to hit her, he simply couldn't shake his desperation to leave her marked. Anyone else who undressed her afterwards would find the parallel bruises he had made, not extreme, but unmistakable. Because apparently he had the right. And, without him, she'd remain his statement – not of ownership, he promised her, but of love. He would bite her for similar reasons and hate that he had to and hate who he was.

'Is there anyone? Emily?'

'No.'

'Look at me, though. Look at me and tell me there's no one else.'

'There's no one else.'

'Call me darling.'

'Darling.'

And that distance in her eyes where she was unreachable and at her loveliest.

I knew there wasn't anybody else, there wasn't honestly even me.

'You could say . . . If you would just say, Emily. It would be all right and I wouldn't be angry. I would just want you to tell me. Because I love you. Emily? You do know that, don't you?'

'Yeah.'

'I love you more than anything, and you're my real wife and you have to know that. You're the one that counts.'

Because she never mentioned love he dropped into harder and harder declarations until he couldn't bear to hear himself, would nuzzle between her breasts and try to be deafened by her heartbeat as it pounced beneath his ear.

'Darling Mark.' The way a child would say it, or someone from another country, testing if they could.

'Darling Emily. Thank you. Darling Emily.'

And when everything else was exhausted, he had to be alone with her and opened. 'I would marry you if you asked. I would try and we could do that. We could. If you wanted. It would be complicated, but if you wanted.'

Although their initial excursions to bars delighted him, he learned he should steer her away from too much booze. Uncontrolled drinking made her bleak. Eventually he limited their rendezvous to the hotels, for her benefit. He did his best to care about her in that way and worried if she came to him unsteady or with her skin under that heavy sheen of previous alcohol. On evenings when she was too out of it, he kissed and held her and no more and was glad to feel her dreams shift in his arms. 'Sweetheart, I have to go now, will you be okay? Are you okay? You should sleep. Keep asleep.'

I wanted to cure her.

I did right by her, almost constantly.

Only that one night when I let myself down. I fell.

I was closing the door, but I wanted to look at her, a parting glance: naked sprawl of my girl across our evidence, the disarray of a cheap fawn coverlet and dull white sheets, her bared feet towards me, plump. She was sleeping it off. She was sleeping me off.

'Night-night, sweetheart.' When I'd kissed her forehead and each closed eye, she'd tasted only pure.

This couple had walked along the corridor at my back and I'd been so absorbed that I hadn't noticed.

And then I did.

And the three of us stood and I knew we were each one of us studying Emily.

I kept the door open – not for terribly long, a breath, a large instant – but I did give that much of her away. And it made me glad. I wanted them to understand that I could touch this angel and she'd got me.

She never knew and it didn't harm her, and then I locked her up safe and the couple moved on.

She was mine, proved mine.

Emily.

He would drive Pauline about – short trips – dance with her or face her at unamusing parties, nod while she talked in supermarket queues, lean near her at the kitchen sink while she washed the dishes and he dried – he did his best to be compliantly domestic when he could – and he would be tight in a fury of needing Emily.

Mine.

Unlike his previous lovers, Emily made him have

increasingly emotional sex with his wife. He would weep
against Pauline's neatly measured breathing and then have
to agree to let her comfort him. His wife as a relief from
the truth of fidelity – it was absurd.

*Like staying in a railway station with no trains that we
can catch.*

Am I displaying hope or idiocy?

*Are we? Or are we pretending this is acceptable, because
we're in company?*

In it together.

A problem shared is not a problem, it's a community.

And so forth.

*We can't claim it wasn't more than possible to foresee
– our likely future.*

The fate of our nation.

And so forth.

*I saw it. I stared at it, sort of, not for terribly long, a
breath, a large instant.*

*Although I suspect my real focus was elsewhere. That's
likely.*

I wasn't alone in ignoring multiple warnings.

Even about trains.

As a student, he had decided he should seem to take an
interest in the wider life. It enriched his social circle.

More girls.

His drive to be committedly well informed meant he'd
attended a lecture by some playwright.

*Face like a punched scatter cushion and a scholarship
boy's accent.*

A laughably earnest audience had squeezed into the
studio theatre at the Barbican Centre and been subjected

to the usual liberal/left stuff – here we are in 1984 and it's ever so much worse than the novel. Smug. The playwright cared. No one could match his extravagant caring, that was plain, and no one else had noticed and resisted the loss of their country's virtue with quite his intellectual elan.

His thesis was okay, though – quite elegant, if repetitive. Probably rehashed it for The Guardian. *That's the way to make money: get paid for saying the same thing, over and over again.*

Sorrysorrysorrysorry.

But I'm the one who pays for that.

The playwright had made frequent and self-consciously lyrical returns to the break-up and sale of the nationalised railways. *Passengers* were no longer *passengers*, they were being redefined as *customers*. *Customers* were happy when they bought something, in this case a ticket. *Passengers* wanted to travel, have politically and economically significant mobility, but instead would have to settle for pieces of thin card and lots of waiting. Dissatisfaction was being rendered inarticulate by a maliciously transformed vocabulary.

Mark had appropriated the idea and used it in arguments whenever he could.

More girls meant I had to find more ways to impress them. Until I could attempt the obvious.

Probably why the playwright was pimping himself onstage.

Both of us aiming to sound insightful and socially engaged.

Which I also aspired to for real.

I was going to be that kind of journalist.

I can't dismiss all my ambitions as just screwing and manoeuvres.

I do like to please people, though. And I'm good at screwing and manoeuvres and that pleases lots of people. Readers don't like insight, engagement, cleverness or any other brands of superiority. They want to feel better and wiser than what they're reading, but they're thick and have low self-esteem, so the bottom of the barrel is where I have to scrape to meet their needs. I worked that out early.

I got a job and made the readers happy.

Making readers happy is not a bad thing.

Readers like screwing and manoeuvres.

Pauline's friends in the ghastly Welsh pub, they were readers. They wanted Westminster gossip – no politics, only the hissy fits and sex. And they were delighted to hear that a minor TV star got guilty with a hooker, racked by the thought of his wife and kids, and please could he limit his one-night stand to a cuddle and then a kip? Innocent. Except the hooker wakes up in the small hours and the star is ejaculating across her back.

I can't tell you his name.

Well, okay then. But don't pass it on.

They adored that. It brought the house down. Pauline something close to proud of me.

She has zero interest in politics. Another reason to marry her. No use washing it out of your work when you get it in your face at home.

I have opinions, of course. I'm not a vacuum. And to find what the readers want, I do have to keep informed. I'm not unable to see that citizens have been recast as customers in every sense and must be content with the act of spending and the blessed receipt of nothing.

Pretty nothing.

Passing trains.

The wider life in which it was at one time sexy to take an interest is not going well.

But I can't be expected to care. And I shouldn't attempt to make other people care, it just screws them up. It's too late for whining and discontent.

And noticing the ruin of others is the quickest way to ruin yourself.

'Please could you?'

It surprised him that Emily didn't also embrace neutrality. It was weird that the matter could even arise.

'Please. You could go with me.'

Because he didn't talk politics with Emily, either.

I didn't want to fake things with her, impersonate a guy who's concerned about refugees, famines. She was smart, had a mind, and I never thought otherwise, but we didn't bother with everyday conversations. We were special. We were busy and beautiful and it would have been an ugly waste of time to disturb each other with crap from the front pages.

We gave each other peace.

So that evening with her was a shock. 'You want me to go on a demo?' A small, nice shock.

'You could. Mark. With me. You could.'

Demonstrations were fashionable amongst her contemporaries – they had been when he was her age, because they looked good and passed the time – but she had a passion here, too. She'd given matters thought.

Passions and thought in my absence.
Unreasonable to be jealous.
But I was.
But I was in glory as well, bathed in the joys of her
having revealed herself in this regard, of her having asked
for something, stated opinions.

'It's wrong – things are all wrong. Once somebody's got more than they need, they don't need more.' Sincerity thrumming on her skin so noticeably that he wanted to lick her.

In fact, he did lick her. 'That's a slogan, though, Sweets. And things are complicated.'

'People say things are complicated when they don't want them to change. No one says heart surgery is complicated, so they won't try it – people want to be alive, so they do it.'

'I think they do say heart surgery's complicated.' Her expression hardened against him when he mentioned this – even though he was smiling. 'Or maybe not now. Maybe it's easy now. No, I know what you mean and that's good. It's a good metaphor. I'll use it.' He leaned himself towards the edge of offending her, bruising her principles, so that he could really feel how wonderful it was that she had them and how wonderful it was that she hadn't completely thrown away her degree. She'd told him that much.

Five or six weeks after we'd started and she'd wanted
to be more to me maybe, to have a little past.

'In sociology?'

After a deep kind of night.

'Yeah.'

Her eyes had been very open and very concerned with his own.

'Wow! Darling.'

'Like you're surprised I got one.'

'Like I'm – no – not surprised . . .' At which point he found himself losing any explanation that possibly her scuffle and drop between service jobs and periods of unemployment had struck him as unsatisfactory, in the sense of being not good enough for her. And it seemed even more a form of self-harm in the light of her having an, albeit laughable, degree. Her mum was a cleaner, her dad was shady and elsewhere, but she had a degree, the usual debt – more than the usual and something else to do with a grandparent's savings – and a degree . . . and a much older boyfriend who didn't want to sound at all paternal. Mark didn't want to suggest that her being with him was another indication of a reckless and damaging life.

'You want me to be different.'

'No, darling. No. My best girl's my best girl. Truly. You have to do what you want.' And he'd kissed her to break the conversation, kept on until they were silence and motion and nothing.

And I held her once we were done for so long that it appalled me.

Her later fixation about the demo had allowed Mark to hear himself repeat, 'You have to do what you want.' Which was true for everyone. 'And I have to do what you want and that's what I want. If you ask – and I like when you ask and you never have asked before, really – then I have to do what you want.'

She gave me a date and a time – an inconvenient date and time – when she would need me.

A breakthrough.

She was breaking through.

It was mainly gorgeous.

And she'd placed a minute kiss against his ear. 'I would like it.' Sober and giggly and energetic. 'I would.' This was Emily showing herself as a credible companion away from the bedrooms. She'd made a promise of ways they might be and he'd accepted it.

I think we both knew that.

'But a demo, baby . . . Not a concert, or an opera, or the movies, or the zoo.' It occurred to him that he could only guess at the majority of her pastimes. She remained largely closed to him. 'Or a club with naked ladies dancing that I would enjoy, but not as much as I enjoy you . . .' Kissing her in return across her stomach. 'I haven't been on a demo since I was a student and that, as we're allowed to mention, is a long, long time ago.'

Emily had shaken her head like a woman who loved him and only couldn't say so because it was too much. 'Not that long. And if you've done it once, then you'll know how.'

It made sense – drunks run their lives backwards: from unintimate intimacy to revealing commonplaces.

He'd had no intention of denying her, but he knew she would like if he teased her. 'Say "Go with me, darling Mark, and make love to me first for at least an hour." Go on.'

'Then you'd have to stay the night.' She offered this as if it were an ordinary sentence and didn't scald his breath and then remove it. 'Because we'd have to set out early. Please, darling Mark.'

Staying the Friday night with her and waking and getting the Saturday morning, too.

If I allowed it, then I'd want it again.

She would start to show on me and I'd like that and let it happen.

Sweet Emily.

I belong to sweet Emily. She's the girl who has broken me. Wide open. You could park your car inside my chest.

Watching her light while she rolls out this story about being kettled and the cops pressing in and it's turning a bit lairy before these kids – she called them kids – start up singing some daft protest song – I can't recall any protest song that wasn't a dirge – and the crowd laughs and the cordon pauses and it's clearly this golden moment for her, proof of something. Hope.

And I wanted her to hope.

My generation is at fault – not active like the one before it, not active like the one behind – and she tasks me with this slightly.

I don't believe that direct action makes any difference, but she did and it was lovely that she did.

Her expectations of happy change were as sexy as fuck.

Emily had kept on, more enthused than he'd known her, while he bled joy and horror invisibly into the sheets. 'Please, darling Mark, and make love to me first. Yeah? Have I asked like you'd like?' She was becoming a woman he'd want in her entirety.

He could have taken out a full-page ad. A Sunday feature. 'Yes, well, okay. Okay.' Her lips parted for him, still sticky with the *darling* that was him translated. His tongue tried to taste the word and failed, because it was given and gone. 'You're a funny girl, bad girl. I'll have to plot like anything, so we can get away with that. Maybe Kempson will let me do colour on the anarchists, or the school kids, or something – *the reality of modern unrest.* He'll tell me what reality he wants: brave and sexy sixth-formers with compassion for the urban poor, or home-grown barbarians who want to piss on war graves and buy anthrax . . . Both . . .'

And this rushing, magnificent lurch in his thinking when he saw her frown, fully display her disapproval. At last.

Because opposition is a proper part of love.

Or maybe I was a pervert: finding a new source of desire because there was finally something I'd done that offended her. And, in recompense, I could utterly apologise, abase myself.

He'd made a point of kneeling, pressing his mouth to her ankles, her feet. Kissing for forgiveness, all bared skin and making himself plain. 'I don't write what I believe, Emily. I should. Probably. But I'm not sure about that.' His words and good intentions at the soles of her feet, plump, grubby. He was being devoted. 'Newspapers aren't something that people take seriously, not now. They're dying.' And hauling this, mining it from his bones, 'I think you could teach me to branch out, though.' Nothing but sincere. 'Maybe I could write a book.'

Nothing, but sincere.

A tingle racing the length of me when she accepted this and grinned.

Funny girl, bad girl, best girl.

'And I'll have to be briefed by the Met – midnight updates, I'd imagine – midnight updates, I'll tell Pauline – so I wouldn't want to head home and trouble her when I'd only clatter off again at dawn . . . That would do me in, so I'd want to avoid it. I would have to stay in town. On site. What if something happened in advance of the main event and I wasn't there?'

'You're good at lying.'

'Ssssh. Not with you. Not ever with you.' This overtaking him for a while, driving him back into bed. Into Emily. Into his love.

Then he let her be and managed, 'I'll get us a nice hotel for it. In Mayfair. Would you like that?'

She had changed and so could I.

'I don't mind.'

'A big bath. We've never been in a bath together.'

'I don't mind.' But her eyes on him and apparently glad about it.

'And, baby . . . If neither of us . . . We could meet early and have a room-service dinner and we could be just us and we'd make lots of love and I'd be as nice as nice to you and you'd be as nice as nice to me and, if you could, would you be able to not drink? Baby? Could you? For me? I'd like if you could be there for me. If I was very nice? I don't insist and it's not a problem . . . Emily? Could you be my sober girl? And we'll talk about what you could wear and . . . Could you not drink?'

As he finished, her eyes were cooler. 'I could do that.'

She did sometimes lie to me.

Not that it wasn't his failure as much as hers.

We had to have wine with our dinner, we are grown-ups, that's what grown-ups do.

And we were grown-ups being as nice as nice, if not nicer.

While he took calls and checked his email she'd hold him. Occasionally she'd sip her wine.

One bottle between us and that was it. Extremely moderate.

Our perfect night.

We didn't sleep.

Any rush about joining the protesters evaporated in a long breakfast with crumbs on the pillows and their skin. They didn't get outside until noon and Mark's concentration was shredded with his body's protest, its missing her, yowling because he wasn't naked and clasping her wants.

'Shit, I'm not . . . Do you mind if we back out a bit and get a long bead on it? We will join the parade in a while, but I've got to get my head straight. Okay, Sweet?'

Piccadilly was thick with marchers when Mark gazed beyond the hotel doors. He was slightly puzzled and slightly moved by the old-school brass bands passing, the embroidered union banners that kicked things back into the 1930s, or the 1970s – those little brackets between which self-respect had probably become a more widespread delusion. It was all making the hotel doormen nervous.

It wasn't a great day to be wearing a top hat.

And 'Not a Good Day to Wear a Top Hat' did indeed appear as my catchline. Set the style – observant, amused, keen not to overestimate the significance of events.

Mark coaxed Emily along to Shaftesbury Avenue and scolded his mind into focus. He was fine by the time a dark knot of angsty figures ran and yelled down the pre-emptively cleared road.

If I was a serious anarchist bent on mayhem I wouldn't dress in black and – oh, grow up – wave a fucking flag.

Police, also dressed in black, moved in sharply around the outskirts of the group and then closed. Emily seemed fascinated by the flag-waver, a skinny twenty-something with a Jesus face.

He wanted somebody to beat him up. Is that what she

wanted in a man, that he should suffer? Would she have wanted to beat me?

I would have let her.

I would have begged.

The Met tested their day's waters, locking into solid ranks. Mark found the whole situation both weirdly childish and horribly serious. It worried him.

I knew the day was going to turn at some point and eat us up. It was going to be bad.

He clasped Emily's arm like an indulgent father squiring his activist daughter.

The solitary time I did that, played that card.

And the police cordon parted, let them through, then dissolved altogether with a carefully presented unconcern. The anarchists bolted off wildly as they might have been expected to. Mark thought their triumph unwise. He kissed the top of Emily's head to cheer himself. Her hair smelled of hotel shampoo.

And of nothing.

'Can we now?' Emily pliant – even daughterly – letting him take charge in a whole new way. 'Can we march?'

My hand around hers, around what was given completely.

She looked at me.

Someone shouting through a loudhailer, and mild chaos waiting for us to join it, but we were a couple. We were really there.

'Yes, babe.' And Mark anxious that he shouldn't cry and also uneasy and too ragged to identify exactly why. 'We'll do it now and we'll get all afternoon together.' He slipped his hold to her waist and squeezed. 'But I'll have to make notes and be . . . and then I'll need to work, flat-out work. I should have sketched some bits down yesterday. It's okay, though. And I'm glad I'm here, and I'm glad I'm with you and it's a good idea.'

Stepping out from the pavement and into the road – that moment – I'd forgotten what it was like.

Hello.

This is me in the world that's different.

This is everyone else.

And this is us.

We are us.

Real.

It wasn't hard to lean against her and be carried, to be shaken loose into enjoying it. She'd point out good bits: a kid in a pushchair with his own hand-made sign, a bunch of blokes in amazing hats playing concertinas. He did the same: the Writers' Guild placards – typographical humour – an old lady near the entrance to Hyde Park who was holding this kind of essay up under her chin; it was unfurled to the ground, as long as herself. It said what her name was and that she was from Tower Hamlets and not happy with the government – who was happy with government? – and Mark didn't read the rest.

Mark had liked the energy: the cardboard tank that pumped out reggae, and he and Emily heading on while all the rage burned by them and insisted on producing a variety of elation and music and

Muzzy fellow-feeling. A consoling fantasy of change.

They all wanted an afternoon stroll to have built Utopia by Monday.

Emily pulled him into the park and there it was as he'd expected – the forward momentum pooled and sank, there

was litter and dirty clothes and Quakers eating shredded
vegetables out of Tupperware containers. He was no longer
uplifted and it was chilly and he'd have been wiser to keep
their room on for another day and look out of the fucking
window – cosy and with Emily – take a nap and then knock
out the story as required.

And he was exhausted suddenly, overwhelmed and achy,
and then he went wrong.

I made her unhappy.

*She wanted me to sit on the grubby turf with her, take
in the scene, listen while the converted doggedly tried to
convert the converted.*

But I'd done that before.

When I was her age.

*I'd already disappointed myself back then and didn't
intend to again.*

So I disappointed her.

Worse.

He'd been – to a minor degree – short with her. She was
laughing and lying on the grass, wriggling like a puppy,
playing a game that he didn't have time for.

'Emily! I have to work. For God's sake!'

I'd never shouted at her.

*Older man in a bourgeois overcoat, screaming at a sweet,
sweet girl, killing her smile.*

*I couldn't seem to bring it back right after that and I
tried.*

I did.

'No, Emily, sweetheart. I'm all messed up. I messed up.
I promise. Forget what I said. I'll stay here. If you want me
to. I'll do whatever you want.' His clumsy, pathetic gestures

wagging and losing themselves in the air ahead of him. 'Baby. I'm sorry. I really am . . .' He wanted to cry for her, but couldn't and knew his face was somehow outwith his control and frightening to her. She fluttered to her feet, harm apparent everywhere, and started out for the road without him. He didn't try to touch her in case he did more harm.

And the brothers and sisters might have pitched in and stopped me if I laid hands on her – nothing more judgemental than a revolutionary. They despised me.

But I beat them to it.

'Let me, please let me be with you.' Remembering he'd said this as he slipped the key card into the lock of their first hotel room. It was a revelation – how abject he had sounded. 'Emily.' Not as abject as today. 'Christ, please.' The fracture in his voice presumably what slowed her and let him reach and hold and find and kiss her better, surely better.

The comrades approved. Solidarity giving rise to love.

Love.

Which was what you would battle to save, and Mark didn't love the unfriendly world, or impractical ideas, or people, he loved Emily. He had marched for Emily and she had made it beautiful for him and he should let go and appreciate that.

And I did. I partly marched again and partly strolled with her back west until the demonstrators coalesced into a stolid mass: rumours and shifting and then cheers.

I stood with everybody else, I stood with Emily – got to keep Emily – got to keep Emily safe – and I watched a bunch of arseholes climbing the front of Fortnum's and I cheered.

They were up there with coloured chalk for scrawling

*and a painted bed sheet for unfurling – more cheers – and
I wouldn't have put it past them to stage some agitprop on
the shop's canopy instead of simply swanning about while
the staff peered out through the windows, amused and
curious.*

*There were rumours – correct – of others storming the
entrance.*

Storming a tea room.

A – rumours again – non-tax-paying tea room.

*Barging inside a posh tea room while badly dressed and
singing some songs. Anarchists in the queen's grocer's.*

A redefinition of storming.

Emily had cheered, too, and made Mark call out louder
until he could feel her voice in his chest. He raised his hands
above the press of bodies as apparently most people had
– taking pictures full of raised hands holding cameras to
take pictures – and a kid was writing TORY SCUM on
Fortnum's wall in what was pretty close to the store's famous
shade of green.

I did wonder if that was intentional.

Eventually Mark slipped round to Emily's back, embraced
her until she was snug and they fitted and were in triumph.

More cheers.

Mark preferred not to wonder why the Met hadn't closed
and confined the whole pack of them. The marchers were
effectively kettling themselves. The police he'd seen along
the route had been chatting in gaggles, lounging, steadily
denying they could exert any kind of control. A paint-
cannon had fired in the distance throughout the morning
– a low threat of sound – windows had been broken, land-
marks were defaced with no reaction.

Mark tried not to guess that night would fall on indulged transgression with no good marching comrades left between it and a hard reassertion of the law.

It would be dreadful.

He wanted to bring Emily into the office and write with her there – she'd be out of harm's way and close and fine – but he wouldn't have got down a word with her about, he had to be realistic. And every passing bastard would have wanted to hear who she was.

I wasn't ashamed of her.

She'd checked in the day before looking like an upmarket secretary – I'd thought that would play well – but when she left the hotel in the morning she was dressed for the demo: fatigues and boots and an ethnic hat – crazy tweed jacket. But it only seemed crazy because it was so big – because it was mine.

Beautiful baby.

On both days.

Sexy.

She'd have knocked the office over and I'd have adored it.

In theory.

'Baby, sweet baby, though. I've gotta go.' His syllables against her neck, being sweet as he could to match her sweet. 'Come with me as far as the Underground. Would you?'

'Don't we have some more time?'

'I can't. Work.'

'I could sit in your office while you work.' She was able to say this, because she'd been close enough to hear his thinking. Naturally.

He'd kept his plans vague and persuaded her to edge

herself free with him and to pick their way, slower and slower, until they found an operational and fairly uncrowded Tube station. Covent Garden again. 'I don't want to leave you, sweetheart. Emily. I don't want to. You're my wife. It's killing me.' At the top of the stairs, he'd ricocheted through his goodbye. 'I'll make it better. Soon. I'll make us all better, just fine.' He'd spoken unwisely.

Holding her head – everything she thought of me – between my hands.

The touch spoke in my palms for hours afterwards. She was there, she was sheathed between the tendons. It made me clumsy. For five- and ten-minute spaces I couldn't type.

By the time he'd hit his deadline, the predictable spasms of violence were breaking out on the streets – resistance against resistance – and he could end the article with a riff on youthful altruism versus betrayal, anger and nihilism and the British tradition of blahblahblah. He'd let the newsier pieces do the rest.

The risk of Emily reading it was low, but I could still feel her being somewhere and frowning at me.

It was a grim trip home – cab driver full of aggressive certainties. Then he'd slipped in beside Pauline after an arduous shower. She mumbled and turned, became still.

He'd wanted to sleep for a decade.

Or just until Monday and then call Emily and work out how to do this again.

He'd left his clothes in a heap by the bedside cabinet.

In my dreams, I unreeled the day, had it again. I sat folded behind Emily in the bath and washing her hair. I made sure the soap didn't get in her eyes.

When Pauline rattled him awake, he struggled to surface.

And I was angry.

I'd been awake for thirty-six hours, high-profile piece to finish under the gun, on my feet, on my back, on my mind – too much for a Burroughs boy.

I was very angry.

And having this knowledge that sometimes a sweet thing can be exhausting.

I was outraged.

Pauline had waited until Mark had opened his eyes. Then she'd hit him.

A slap.

Just one.

Passed me my phone, which I hadn't turned off to preserve my privacy and hadn't tucked away.

I'd been too tired to be sensible.

Only that once.

Which was enough.

More than enough.

As he took the phone from Pauline, he'd understood who would be calling.

Emily.

Very drunk.

Emily.

Very explicit and drunk.

Emily.

In hospital for reasons she couldn't make plain.

Emily.

She couldn't make much plain.

Emily.

She told me she loved me.

Emily.

Almost inaudible.
Emily.
She told me she wanted to be my wife now.
Emily.
Almost inaudible.
Emily.
I couldn't go and get her.
Emily.
Almost inaudible.
Emily.
I couldn't do what she wanted.
Emily.
Almost inaudible.
Emily.
I couldn't explain.
Emily.
Almost inaudible.
Emily.
She ought to have understood.
Emily.
Almost inaudible.
Emily.
I'd asked her to be my sober girl and she'd let me down.
Emily.
She'd let me down very badly.
Emily.
Almost inaudible.
Emily.

It was funny the way he could hear it all more clearly now – remembering on a hopeless railway platform and too late.

It was not funny that Pauline could always tell when he remembered. Endlessly well attuned to his impulses and reflections and perpetually suspicious, Pauline was his daily penalty to pay. If he thought of Emily, just the dab and graze of Emily's name, then Pauline could tell.

And I want her to tell. I show her.

Scars of ownership.

They make you.

His wife was currently facing him, her expression suggesting that he was an unhealthy animal and ought to be destroyed.

A view with which I must concur.

Mark felt the drum of an oncoming locomotive, before he could hear it. The sensation was not unlike excitement.

Excitement being something without which I have to do.

There were conditions he had to meet if he wanted to stay with Pauline.

Which I'd rather not, but I seem to have no choice.

I can't think of a choice.

On the night of Emily's call – the early morning of Emily's call – he'd fled to a hotel – King's Cross, but nowhere familiar. Pauline had kept his phone.

But he could still have rung Emily back, he could have.

He didn't, though.

It was impossible.

Each time he tried to, he couldn't ring her, and each time it became harder to try.

And if Emily had called his phone again, Pauline never said so.

Well, she wouldn't.

There was nothing left.

And he hadn't wanted one wife and he'd never wanted two. Only love – he'd wanted love, needed love, would have died for love. But Emily hadn't wanted that.

She wanted me, but not my love – that was the wisest opinion to cultivate.

So I went back to my presentable London postcode, loft extension, male Polish au pair with a marine-biology degree. And Pauline bought me a new phone – not pink – and she checks the numbers on it now and then, the way she checks my diary, and she calls the office and checks me. Her new career is keeping tabs on me and I can have no women and no girls and I can't flirt at social gatherings and everyone knows I was caught and maybe most of the details, I don't enquire, and everyone knows I am finished and done with, because they can see it, and I ought to be okay with this because I deserve it, but I am not and I ought to find satisfaction in the fact that I'm so blatantly chained and watched, because it marks me as a man who was prodigious and is a public demonstration of my prior capacities, but I'm not okay.

I'm not happy.

Mark smiled at Pauline, kept it insincere, because she suspects him when he seems to have a meaning.

But I do sometimes, not for terribly long, a breath, a large instant, believe that I am being hurt for Emily, suffering and being punished for Emily and that she would want it.

It makes us close.

Pauline had cleansed his address book, wiped dozens of numbers.

But I know Emily's number by heart. I gave it to her.

The air sealed itself as the train receded, burned by and left them like a spasm of rage.

One day I will call her.

I will.

Hello.

This is me, this nothing.

Hello.

Hello.

Hello.

Takes You Home

He would have preferred it if anyone else had been dealing with this, coping with this. This was the kind of stuff you dealt with and coped with when somebody died – somebody other than yourself. That was Mike's opinion, although he had no one to hear it unless he started blurting out to strangers, which wouldn't aid his case in most directions so he kept schtum.

I haud my wisht. I haud it tight.

He'd noticed these playground colours of speech nudging back in at him lately.

Like as if I was still wee, then I'd be fine. Because I'd no be worried. I widnae fash.

Mike didn't quite know how to view this new interior development. He supposed it was vaguely reassuring, allowing in the ghost of his previous voice, a cosy accompaniment to his lists of tasks outstanding and general frets. But equally, the implications were all a bit sodding desperate if he really did want to be a boy again and helpless, because no one was going to take care of him at this point. No one was equipped.

And anyway a child couldn't manage a serious worry,

a child would be destroyed. That's the reality on which to focus, probably.

Or not. Maybe not.

He stared out at how mean-looking his spare room was: grubby and with scrapes to the paintwork and dirty lines left on the walls since he'd taken down the pictures. It gave the impression he'd lived in a slovenly manner. The whole situation rendered more dismal by the yellowish frown of an eco-friendly bulb.

Bloody things are never that keen about turning on – have to ease themselves into the effort over a period of hours. They're the elderly aunts of the lighting world.

He'd packed up the lampshades already.

Few things sadder than a shadeless lamp.

Unless it's an unattended wean.

Which I am not and shouldn't imagine that I am – it'll make me depressed.

Still, though.

I can't deny that folk take care of weans. They wouldn't leave a child in cruel rooms, or jaggy circumstances.

He swiped up at the bulb, caught it with his fingertips and set it to swing and splash shadows against each wall.

This proving I'm a big wean.

Walks in as John Wayne, crawls out as a big wean.

That's how they used to put it. In the youthful circles I was warned not to frequent, because then I'd learn how to speak in a style that was Not Nice.

Mum imagined the wind would change, or something, and I'd be stuck sounding inappropriate forever. Didn't want me showing the household up as Common in her Nice Street. So I couldn't say I was a wean, although I was a wean, unless I was away off with other weans and had no Nice adults around who'd get affronted and step in to adjust me. She didn't appreciate that I could vary: I could sometimes be a wean and sometimes a child who lived in the west of Scotland and yet maintained an aspirational accent at some social cost.

Truthfully, I didn't vary well – I never could sound flaw-lessly Nice in Nice settings, because it felt like lying, and meanwhile and elsewhere the taint of Niceness had crept in about me nonetheless and leaked through to bugger up my sentences when I was trying to relax in Less Nice company.

What did me in was the family relocating east. To the Nice Side of the Country, I was assured.

I shifted with them, Mum and Dad – what else would I do? I was eleven then and not exactly free-standing.

But I never quite got round to picking up an eastern accent. I didn't even try.

I never respoke a wean into a bairn.

I settled for sounding foreign – or up myself and smug, as I was often assured – and didn't bother much with friends. I buckled under and scrambled up the aspirational ladder. I pleased my mum. I think I pleased my dad. I think I didn't care if I pleased me, although I shouldn't complain – the ladder's barely there, these days.

But I didn't love it. The constant demands for further climbing gave me vertigo. And all it amounted to finally was earning my very own cubicle and keyboard and being left to find the joy in expressing others through the medium of maths. Then I got an office and more of the same. I sat in my office and oversaw needs and people and how they might best be described. I did not meet the people. I did not necessarily meet the needs. My job was to be the kindness of strangers. Or not. I varied.

Another reason for keeping quiet, hauding the wisht.

Which I am, by now, good at. I haud it with both hands and squeeze until it gets no air and I am silence.

Although he did currently want to make a remark, perhaps in the hearing of someone sympathetic.

I would say – if the opportunity presented, which it doesn't – that I am being compelled to put my affairs in order, which has a bad sound. It's not aspirational.

He'd have added a comment or two on the way life had been for the last few weeks, or months.

It's been a year.

Maybe he was noble, to some degree, for putting up with it. He'd considered this, but dismissed the idea because he'd seen better behaviour in other contexts and courage was only real, anyway, when someone else was watching. Then it occurred to him the truly noble act nobly with no one there to see and this meant perhaps he qualified, because he was unseen. Perhaps he was slightly admirable. The only certain thing was that he felt nauseous most days and as if he mustn't slow, or stop moving until exhaustion dropped him, because otherwise he knew he'd have to cry.

I do persevere, you can't fault me on that account.

And I have gone to my place of residence and am putting my affairs in order. Which used to be a sign of ill omen in the kind of British films they no longer make, ones that showed chaps in suits, or chaps in uniforms, or – at a pinch – chaps who wore suits for Sundays and were working-class and ill-kempt otherwise, but also Nice. Everyone had noticeable consonants. And in would come the dreadful news from the doctor who'd wear a waistcoat with his suit and side-whiskers, or else the shock would spring from a letter revealing some fatal disgrace. Or one of the chaps – in his uniform, or suit, or Nice Sunday Best of appropriate period – would clip out deftly structured phrases, explaining to some other chap that he was in trouble, insolubly so.

Next would be a show of dignity: compressed working-class dignity, repressed middle-class dignity, suppressed upper-class dignity, and then came the ordering.

Dear chap, I will have to go now and order my affairs.

Mike was unclear about what the phrase properly meant, beyond the imminent removal of the chap from his affairs and the looming end of comforts and contentments of every type for solely awful reasons. It also seemed to imply that a real man should leave substantial effects behind him: a catalogue of family mementoes, letters bound with ribbon and medals from appalling wars, an orderly trove of stored wounds. It ought to be taxing to order his things, because a man should produce a legacy, at the very least of secrets honourably kept and kind regards.

I've none of that.

Or, ideally, a man was a man of substance and had an estate with dependent cottages, fishing rights, a manor with a slew of ballrooms, livestock and portfolios, diamonds, the newer of the Bentleys he'd leave to the wife.

I'm not leaving anything to the wife.

Mike was, in fact, simply leaving. He was letting his withdrawal run its course, combing through every material proof of himself and either abandoning it, or tamping and taping it down into cardboard containers. He had

– and this wasn't startling – proved to be of unimpressive substance. There were also too many items he couldn't stand the sight of, as it turned out, so he was chucking most of them.

I might have kept more if I'd got hold of tea chests for storage. I remember them as being reassuring.

When I was a kid, Mum and Dad still had a few up in the loft from when they'd finally arrived at Windsor Gardens, their Nice Street in the east. Their pinnacle of Niceness. Neither of them ever had to pack up and move on after that. They abandoned their responsibilities in the traditional order – him first and then her – and each of them was carried out, boxed and beyond caring, by Nice Undertakers. Then the house was cleared.

By me.

Nicely.

So I've done this before and should have been spared.

Or at least if I'd searched out tea chests to keep me company for this bit – proper wooden boxes that smelled of exotic places and quality cuppas – then I'd have been happier, I think. I'd have believed I was surviving.

Mike remembered the chests as having interesting labels and stencilled marks and strips of thick metal foil protecting their edges. When he played with them, he had to be careful the foil didn't cut his fingers.

I wasn't careful. Naturally.

Blood everywhere. Naturally.

So deep it didn't hurt. Two stitches at the hospital on the last occasion and then lectures about the appropriate levels of caution to maintain if I was to manage myself as an adult operation.

Crying into my mother's cardigan until she stopped scolding.

I never intended to grow up and have to be adult.

But I did. Naturally.

Although I've heard it said on several occasions that I simply got taller and faked the rest.

I've heard that said with affection.

Around Mike were rafts and walls built out of bland cardboard. His removers had supplied the containers: nothing about what they brought him suggesting terraced hillsides under extravagant heats and skies. And nothing involving effort on his part. This was how grown-ups handled things.

Tediously.

He wasn't taking to it.

But I'm getting through. Like a sterling individual, a fine chap.

Or rather, he wasn't. He was spending increasing periods trying to be some other person, further off. There was a fairly constant pressure inside his flat which combined the stresses of heavy lifting with those of unearthing familiar objects and their more or less savage echoes, with noticing cracks in the plaster and the eradication, in some way he couldn't fathom, of his hope. Becoming other than himself had relieved this and allowed him, more or less, to prepare his home for sale and then himself for his removal. He was, if not a kind stranger, then competent.

I am getting through.

I am doing so as another man who looks and sounds impostorish, but is better than me, and that is okay. I've rarely cared how I look and always sounded like an impostor, so none of this matters. It's minor details. I'm a minor detail here.

Sometimes, mostly at night, traces of his personality, spasms and fears, rub between his brain and the interior curve of his skull. This was how he visualised the process. And he was almost convinced that the bones which protected his thinking, which allowed it a moist and warm security, were being worn away exactly and precisely by that thinking.

I mourn the passing of my thoughts.

And, whoever I am, this has been frankly a right pain in the arse and everywhere else.

No one to care except me, but even so.

Throughout his autumn he had stayed in most evenings. This wasn't unusual for him, but seemed an imposition when enforced. He'd been waiting for viewers to come and see his flat – as advertised with a fair degree of honesty in the customary ways. Mike had decided his home should be set beyond his reach and lived in without him, or his ornaments, or his dust.

He hadn't warmed to the prospective purchasers. For one thing, they knew they were in a buyers' market and could therefore act like jaded princelings and empresses.

They were a pack of weirdies.

They said that my windows were peculiar, in the wrong place, an unfortunate shape, needed cleaning, were painted a gloss white that wasn't quite gloss or white enough.

They would plod up the stairs as if I had put every tread in their way to be trying. How else did they want to reach the fourth floor? With a bosun's chair, on a pack mule, hauled aloft by servants of their retinue . . .?

And then they would tell me, 'It's dark.'

Course it was dark; they only ever came after sunset and that's when it tends to get dark and why we have candles and torches and eco-friendly light bulbs and it's why we buy table lamps in the shape of nude women with tensed bodies and long 1930s' hips.

I've wanted one of them for years, since I was barely beyond a wean.

The setting of the sun is why we bothered to have the Industrial Revolution: we wanted to keep out the badness of the night.

We don't like badness. We can't stand the way it is worse than being blinded, how it paces and howls with fears.

He clapped his hands for no particular reason, beyond a need to hear something in his rooms. The CD player and, indeed, the CDs and old cassettes and saved vinyl and every part of his music had been jettisoned. This seemed a better idea every day: since his belongings had retreated into huddles, the whole place sounded peculiar and would have screwed up his tunes if he'd let them loose in it.

Once a tune's gone bad you can't save it.

This way the whole place hauds its whisht. I have my reasons.

He scuffed through to the kitchen. His inadequate kitchen, apparently.

The viewers wanted it up-to-date. But why would I bother with that? What if they found my blatantly new kitchen was also repellent? Then it would be more convincingly wrong than the knackered one that's here, and which only quietly asks to be replaced and will shrug when it's knocked to pieces and hauled away and not take it personally one bit.

Likewise with the bathroom – they all despised it.

But it isn't poky. It has never been found poky by those

whose judgement I respect. Two people can manage well in that bathroom simultaneously. Three or four could be accommodated, but who would want that, who would need that? No one.

He'd had to agree there was an issue with the shower curtain.

Can't avoid seeming infectious, an unknown shower curtain. You stand and draw it across, close across, and you worry about the marks on it and what they might imply and, should it be spotless, you still freak out when it brushes you, possibly where it has brushed other bodies before. It has memories of contact which disturb.

But if I'd taken it down, then the bath would have looked too naked and as if I shower without protection and am odd and have exposed my joists and floorboards to hazardous levels of damp.

Someone didn't like the boiler. A man with stained ear-hair and ugly glasses looked at it askance.

I looked at him askance.

It's a new boiler. Newish. It is serviced. On its left-hand side is a printed sticker recording maintenance dates and showing signatures to prove that all has been repeatedly well, or mended and tended until it was well.

The sticker is almost full of tinily noted visits by trained personnel, mostly in the scribbly writing of the young engineer who's usually sent by the servicing company and who also checks the gas fire.

He once found a pigeon, dead at the back of the fire. I hadn't heard it being trapped or dying, but there it was. Unfortunate. I liked to think it had pegged out quickly. Birds can die of simple horror, they're frail that way. I had to bring in a pan and brush and washing-up gloves and hand them over before the guy would make a start on removing the little body, the maggots. He appeared likely to spew, although he held himself back, which was good of him.

I could have tidied up myself – both the pigeon and, for that matter, any spew. I'm not squeamish, but I didn't volunteer. Why pay a dog to visit and then piss on the carpet yourself?

Which isn't a good way to put it, is coarse and inaccurate, but then I am. Lately, this person who I am is boorish.

The servicing guy has changed, too. Each time, he gets thicker in his neck and face. As if he's maturing outwards in rings, as a tree would.

One viewer had a problem with the gas fire, too – didn't fancy its general attitude and demeanour.

Mike wondered if it had an atmosphere of doom about it, a sense that blowflies might ease their way horribly out from the dark behind it and have to be murdered each morning.

That happened for a while. Three or four flies in the living room each dawn, banging at the windows to get out and find further meat.

None of them prospered in the long term.

Then it stopped.

Mike was already sitting on his sofa before he realised that he'd wandered into the living room. He got up again and faced the fly-hampering windows and then kind of folded. He eased down onto the floor and came to rest with his back against the wall. The window glass was blank, night-filled, curtainless.

His armchairs were here with him, huddled in a knot. One might guess they were chatting and didn't wish to be disturbed.

He was tired.

And he was heavy-handed. This had endured – his ability to break things and be bewildered in his fingers. He rested his knuckles on the carpet as if he were setting down stones.

Van comes in the morning, hauls everything into storage. What's left.

It would be none of his business when, in the afternoon, a couple would show up and open his door with the keys that were presently hiding in his coat pocket.

Then they'll let themselves in and they'll let themselves in.

He wasn't going to wait for them, because that would be peculiar.

He wasn't going to say they ought to leave the kitchen as it is, because it has warm work surfaces which are good for making bread, and that loaves had been baked in its oven regularly and had smelled like love and been only beautiful to come home for.

He wasn't going to mention that they shouldn't repaint the walls – the scruffy, unimpressive walls – because they were important. The last time they were painted, he'd taken a week off to do it and so had Margaret and they'd uniformed up in cheap blue overalls. Hers were enormous on her: sexy, baggy, rolled at the ankles and wrists – smooth, fine ankles and wrists – and clearly there was a sense, a true sense, a provable, testable sense, that she was naked and shifting and warm there and surprising and understood – by him understood – and just there, so there, inside them.

She was extremely there inside them. God bless all women with long 1930s' hips.

So deep it didn't hurt, never hurt, did not hurt anyone ever. We were the opposite of hurt.

And they'd bought themselves brushes, rollers, paint trays, paint and other practical gifts and they'd cleared and covered what they wanted to stay clean and so there was nothing to do but the fun part – starting in.

With music.

They tried different types.

R&B was good, it often suited, and sometimes they went slipping down the seam between it and the blues, pure blues.

So they hadn't painted, they had danced.

One week of dancing.

And the work rolled on, smooth with the rhythms, room after room, no effort, just heat. Easy. Although they'd complain in the mornings: stiff shoulders, tender backs; before the beats kicked up and Ray Davis helped them, Aretha Franklin helped them, C.W. Stoneking helped them, the early Stones helped them and the late Stones helped them and Justin Timberlake helped them and the Black Eyed Peas helped them. They had a lot of help, in fact – they kept it successfully varied.

They worked up a sweat. They got happyweary until it was evening and time to put on Simon and Garfunkel – a folky exception to their rules and suitable for winding down – and they'd lean back against songs that sounded unconsoled and broken, but happy with it. They made everything seem fine and mildly transcendent. Perfect.

Once the bridge had gone over the troubled water, Mike set the brushes to soak and cleaned the rollers and Margaret would unveil the room, be dramatic as she whisked back dustsheets and tore away masking tape.

Then they'd smile. Then they'd pause. Then they'd have to get tidy themselves, because that was simply necessary, anything else would be uncivilised.

They'd trot off to be with each other in the shower and search for signs of paint, get scrubbed down to new pink and as clean as weans and as grown as grown and lovely. This running of joy along their skin.

On their last day, he'd told her that they ought to start again, give themselves a new profession, be a couple who painted their flat forever, who'd hook and roll and sidestep for each other. He wanted to mainly spend his life making shapes to entertain her and watching her make them back and feeling her take it home, right home, right home for him.

But they did declare it over and finish. She said she felt wiped out the following afternoon, seriously exhausted, which was their first clue. Maggie didn't seem quite right to herself from then on.

And the doctors agreed when she saw them. She wasn't quite right.

And after that was badness.

Night.

And I can't stand it.

I can't.

So leave the flat.

Please.

Leave the flat alone.

Please.

Keep what's left of us safe without me, because I can't

stay, because it was lovely, because I'm asking. You won't hear, but I'm still asking.

Because Maggie was the kindest person I ever met.

She was where I used to live.

Please.

The Effects of Good
Government on the City

Eventually he's going to say it: 'You don't love me any more.' You can see it in him – a panicky, bleaty light about his eyes – and a couple of times he's actually started the sentence.

'You don—'

It's not that you interrupt him because he's wrong – you can't actually remember if he's wrong. It is true that you didn't think of him especially while you were away. Then again, you thought of no one especially while you were away.

There'd been nowhere for thinking while you were away. Close the doors and draw the blinds and block the chimney, that was the sensible best when you'd been out there.

Not that they'd had really any chimneys out there. Not the way she was used to.

'You don—'

You don't mean him any harm. You wonder if you should tell him, for example, *Stay on known safe areas. Avoid verges.* This is good and accurately retained information, but may not be applicable from his point of view.

He is making you tense and perhaps attempting to bring on a confrontation.

'You don—'

You don't have clarity. It is unclear – no, it is *uninteresting* whether you love him – and your main aim at the moment should be simply to prevent the argument and the ending.

You can't break up with him here.

Not in Blackpool.

You don't want to break up with anyone in Blackpool.

You don't want to be in Blackpool and commit an act you may at some later date recall. Not anyone, not anything, not at any time, not in Blackpool.

That should be the rule. Your rule.

What happens in Blackpool shouldn't.

Not in Blackpool.

Not in fucking Blackpool.

So hard to keep other determinations steady, but you're glad you can be sure that if Blackpool has touched a thing, then the taint will stick. This is a *macabre consideration.* There's someone you trained with who'd put it like that and where they've ended up since then you've no idea, not where you did, not where you have, that's sure certain. It's *macabre* but bloody funny, sort of, to picture yourself in your death's hour, your own death's moment, and your inner eye, you discover, ends up full of that postcard view of Blackpool Tower. That would be a joke. You'd lie there remembering sterilised milk and over-stewed tea – daytime here tastes of that – and if it wasn't the Tower you'd see your boyfriend's face, only not romantic. And they'll watch you – whatever observers are there – and they'll possibly guess you are staring at inrushing angels, heaven's glare, but it'll be all Blackpool stuff you're seeing and you'll want to piss yourself laughing and explain, but no chance there.

This is good, excellent – so much to hate in Blackpool, such a focus. *Focus is essential for operational efficiency.*

The beach here doesn't even smell of beach – it's got that particular stink of small houses where they fry too much. You're right by it, a real sea with the wrong smell and this pretend shoreline, you're on the sand and walking beside the cold of these huge concrete tidal defences – giant steps like something left over from the Reichstag, something bloody vicious, something you'd fabricate to stop a car bomb, an assault.

Is that what they're expecting? An assault? A landing? Amphibious craft and reckless foes swarming in towards Louis Tussaud's?

There's a man up there with a high-pressure hose, wiping the algae and the seaweed off the steps. It'll take him days. And when he moves on he doesn't leave them really clean. Rubbish job, so why bother doing it well? Or maybe that's his best attempt, right there – doing everything he can with what he's got, maximum effort and nobody's right to criticise. The observer can never tell.

Not that you're observing, you're flat-out staring at him – no reason to do it, but also no reason to stop – and you're stuck in between the concrete and the poisoned wave tops on this dead-flat sand and the Central Pier's behind you and the South Pier's up ahead. Hemmed in, as you might consider it. The South Pier being the Scum Pier, apparently, and the North somehow more sophisticated about its slots and tuppenny falls and kiddies' rides and variety shows involving people you thought were long gone, sewn up years ago and nailed underground to stop them corralling the biffs and pensioners and heroes returned home and singing at them, or dancing, or doing tricks, or cranking out gags to please, or maybe all of the above.

Quite probably all of the above. Some of these people are highly versatile – annoying the arse off you in bags of ways.

Vince Hill's here. My dad likes him. Vince Hill 'singing and answering questions'. Bet he never thought he'd end up doing that. Questions. About what?

The whole of your childhood's telly is still here. Hard to be sure which side of the equation is the one in hell: the waxworked entertainers or yourself.

But you would notice, wouldn't you? If you were in hell.

The Central Pier is said to be, just as it ought, somewhere in the middle when it comes to the style and tenor of its diversions.

Trust Blackpool never to miss the obvious.

And the boyfriend, too.

He's looking at you – easy to tell without having to check, because his attention is tangibly leaking, scampering down the side of your face. Fair enough, your boyfriend's supposed to pay heed, but his payment feels like a trickle of something sad. Or as if he's spitting on you.

It is offensive to be spat at, a provocation in many cultures.

He does, of course, want you to be happy here and to accept the blousy, big-grinning town in the proper spirit. He'd like you to join in – this is absolutely the capital of joining in and being of an age when fake plates of bacon and egg made from peppermint rock should prove hilarious, or tasty, maybe even a proof of magical undercurrents in your world.

When you were little here it was all sweet undercurrents. Recalling your childhood unleashes your capacity for wonder, appreciation of kindness and belief. Returning someone to their child self will cause an increase in their potential depth of helplessness and fear. The shock of capture, prolonged, can assist in usefully producing this effect.

Half the shops are selling cocks made of rock now. Or sticks with filth written through them. This isn't for the kiddies and families any more. It's for lap dancers and being on the lash, and sick lights squirming down flat in the rain and being with the boys, except you can't, you've got to watch that – they forget you're not a boy, or else they remember and both are No Bloody Chance in the end. You are not one thing and not the other. You are not most things. You have been somewhere in which most things are not most things and no one gives a toss so why should you and how would you know you ought to and this is how you've ended up.

Bad enough, but then you talked to a milk-white lawyer. Afterwards, he hated you more than anyone, even though you did nothing. You did nothing. That was the point. You did nothing in every way. Nothing about the goings-on, the box of frogs clusterfuck of what was going on.

You did nothing. Then you talked. And you didn't mention the well-meant but turned-out-badly rugby tackles and honest self-defence, because that was bollocks and you were sick of it. You did not speak as agreed.

By the end, with the lawyer and the lawyer's people, there was contempt. You were doing them a favour and that's how they repaid you.

'Are you tired?' Weak boyfriend has to ask something, so he picks a weak question, one you won't block.

'No, I'm not.'

'Are you sure? You look tired.'

This is unsurprising because you do not sleep and, for the last three days, he has been with you and found that out. It is easy to imagine that your wakefulness disturbs him.

'You've got these big shadows under your eyes.'

Lack of sleep cannot be underestimated as a modifier of behaviour and personality. The truth will out.

Easier to imagine your sleep has crawled away from you during the dark and infected him, slid into his pillow and filled him with your dreams. It is Sunday – he looks at you differently today – not the way he did on Saturday or Friday.

'Are you listening?'

You offer him, 'What?' Because you want to delay him, give him another go, so he can change direction.

'I said you seem tired . . .' He pushes an unmistakable amount of misery into his following, trailing silence while he scrambles about for other words, ones that you'll like. 'I thought this would be nice for you. A holiday . . . To get away . . .' He keeps putting you in charge of conversations, choices, directions. You would rather he did not. You would rather be without responsibility.

Still, you'd wanted to leave the village, the cottage, he's right about that. As soon as you were back there you'd noticed the spiders and they'd worried you. Everyone said the weather had been wet for the whole of the summer and autumn – floods in the lower valleys and warm, unremitting rain, damp plaster in your old bedroom's ceiling.

Not your old bedroom – it's just still your bedroom. No one else's.

For some reason these conditions had bred up spiders, fat-bodied and numerous, an infestation your father had failed to mention in his letters. They hung in the corners of doorways and from lamp posts, traffic signs, window frames, in the dark of shrubs and hedges. They bobbed and fidgeted, a sense of unnatural weight about them. Your dad didn't seem to mind – almost gave the impression he had somehow encouraged them, let them colonise the fading raspberry canes and the beans, the shed, the chicken coop. For some reason, the chickens didn't eat them – perhaps this breed was venomous to some degree.

And he let them go into your bedroom. You killed four. Killed them for making it different when it should have been the same.

So you'd cut short your visit, left a bag to show you'd be back, indicate affection, and off to Blackpool with the boyfriend.

Stupid word – he isn't a boy and isn't a friend.

But Blackpool is also inaccessible to lawyers and questions, just as Cyprus will be. And Cyprus is renowned for causing service personnel to get innocent and forget, I'm told. And this is a good thing for everyone, I'm told.

You and your not-boyfriend are currently facing each other – no idea how that happened – and he is very visible, but you realise that if you reach out you won't touch him, he'll be further than the moon, than hell's arsehole, than the back of your mind in the mornings, although this is not his intention.

'Do you want to go? Will we pack up and . . . there are other places . . .'

Like Cyprus.

In the distance beyond him there are three dark shapes, thin men standing and angled perfectly into the breeze, the slack little gusts that taste of dirty washing and stale fat.

They stick on your skin, the oily scents, because of the oil that you have on yourself, the greasiness of being human.

First time you went into the Castle, that's what you noticed – the human reek. Made you gag. Nowhere else was like it: not a tent, not the broil of a Saracen, not the scared wet heat that you leave with your clothes.

You bring it outside on yourself when you leave, the stink, and it doesn't go and you know each other by it – the ones who are your kind – you would know them in the dark.

It is sometimes very dark.

Back and forth from your block to the Castle and the Castle to your block. Noises dragging at your ankles. You didn't like it. You imagined your footsteps laid down as if they were sacking and wet and guilty and layering up.

Guilt is triggered by proximity – over the line and you're too near them and you don't know who should ask the questions, them or you. You've both done stuff, everyone has done stuff – nobody clean over there, and blink and it gets all mixed up. Get in first and then you're safe, it's the order that makes everything. Keep the order and keep angry and then you'll be cooking by gas – that's what you've observed. That's what you're not forgetting, although you will, of course you will.

Your boyfriend is confused. This is your fault, because for a while you liked Blackpool, it was a buzz. You have misled him: first when you arrived you thought the town was fine and this afternoon it's not. Up at the swaying top of the Tower and holding hands while you stood on that little square of clear plastic, the one that lets you peer down at the streets between your feet – that was okay. And shunting each other at the dodgems wasn't bad: the two of you by yourselves, chasing round and round, because the season's over and no one else is playing any more. That electric tang when you swallowed, those spiky little flowers of noise, you would have preferred to skip them. But being one of two adults trying to laugh and yell and get happy, that was okay, a bit mong but okay. And having an Olde Time photo taken together, you couldn't think why you shouldn't. They gave you a dress that fitted in silly places, because you're lean and also muscular and not an average customer. You have grown into the shape the job requires.

The boyfriend who isn't is keeping a copy for when you've left again – straight backs, you're good at that, and sepia, an aspidistra on a table – and you will throw your copy away, because in Cloppa Castle it will not make sense.

After the photo you were discontented and anxious for candy floss because that has a reliable, unoffending smell. You ate toddler-blue spun sugar until your teeth hurt so that it could be a part of you, a place you'll dip into later, but it did not cure you. And you went back to the Tower Ballroom and watched the old, old couples creeping and sliding about to the jaunty organ medley – 'Pack Up Your Troubles' – and this did not help you. Pairs and pairs of people.

Pressure may be usefully applied or threatened against relatives and partners.

Same angles bent in their spines – and here they are dancing, wrapping each other around and high heads and big smiles and if you get to their age you still won't know the steps. You don't believe in dancing. It makes the body visible and is an invitation. It is reckless.

Ended up in a club last night. No dancing. Not the music for it. Red lights darting about in rods and slices, a bit of smoke, and a skinny, big-lipped guy on the karaoke singing 'Nellie the Elephant' – sweating and screaming it.

You nearly laughed at that. Nasty crowd in the place. Nothing in the look of them, in their bearing, that you could like. But you nearly laughed anyway, because 'Nellie the Elephant' all the way through, that gives you your chest compressions and then the two breaths and then again.

FFD and pressure – Dressing soaked – Hemcon – Hemcon – Bleeding not controlled – FFD and direct pressure.

Training for injury.

For when their hearts stop.

And somebody doesn't want them to.

An observer.

Just Another Fucking Observer.

Boyfriend would like to see your eyes – everyone always wants that, point of contact, proof of humanity – but you've got on your new Inks – no sun, but the glasses anyway because you express yourself better in their dark.

Sometimes very dark.

He has seen you, thinks he understands you naked.

Standard Operating Procedure – the utility of nakedness – necessary – you did ask – necessary – make them sing 'Nellie the Elephant'.

When you observe strangers they seem cautious, bundled, prudish. They should be skin and singing – Standard Operating Procedure.

You take off your glasses, show willing, show something, the colour of your thought, a shade that he won't recognise, won't understand. Standard Operating Procedure.

And you're nearer to the standing men by this time – except it appears they're actually cormorants: three birds and not three men. Completely unforgivable you'd get this wrong. They don't like you being so close and fit themselves into the air, long heads and lizard necks pointing into the whitewashy sky.

Nice to hop up like that – leave.

You smile for them and he misunderstands and smiles back and you stroll him in under the pier – repetitions of metal, verticals, diagonals, bad repairs – slush of surf to your right and mercury pools seething in the hollows and at the pillars' feet. The rust is so established it has bloomed into purples, oranges, greens – wide flaking bruises that look infectious, predatory.

This is a not pleasant or secure location and you should leave it.

You lead him up to the pier entrance, wear your glasses again, smile again as you go through the gate and onto the boards.

Some of the wood is soft-rotted, unreliable underfoot, which is amusing although you couldn't explain why.

In Cloppa Castle it is slidey underfoot.

You have special notebooks you can write on when it's wet. Could write on them underwater. You don't have to be underwater. That's not a problem that will afflict you, ask things of you, demand.

The notes you take can sometimes seem absurd and surprise you when you look at your hand writing, your handwriting and the words you continue to find in testing situations.

On the pier, there's a dart game, an old-fashioned scam. You have to chuck darts into playing cards to win a shit prize of this or that sort, or else to win nothing. The cards are pinholed and warry, they seem to have taken hits, which encourages, is intended to draw you, and the stallman, boothman, whoever, gives you a patter which makes it clear that he knows you are military, has noticed it on you although you are not wearing anything approaching uniform because this gets you stared at in the street. Come home and be hated by strangers in the street, avoided by the women in the village who are gathering shampoo and shaving things and affection for returning heroes only. You are not exactly that.

The boothman does not hate you. He lies to you in ways that mean he can steal very small amounts of money for a rigged game and a bit of a chat and a consolation prize of playing cards – made in China – you'll take them with you. If you had darts, you could set up a game of your own. This is perhaps what occurs always – that the scam is passed along from one to another and either harms a little or a lot and that's how we know time is passing, by the progress of each lie – set them free and let them run.

Take the cards back to the Castle.

Where we play many, many games. Shoeing and beasting and whatelsewouldyoulikefromus games making use of the objects to hand.

A childish place, the Castle – even its name – they took it from this 70s' show on the box – Cloppa Castle – puppets and a theme song that warned you'd be staying a while.

You didn't believe it.

First day.

Hoods on the men, but they're naked and singing the theme song.

Fucking mad house.

So you go fucking mad.

What a lily-white lawyer wouldn't understand.

It was hard to explain how annoying you eventually found it when you ordered up the singing from them – they could all speak English, everyone can speak English – and the prisoners sounded scared when you wanted them sounding angry, or sounded angry when you wanted them sounding scared, or when they were faking tiredness, illness. Or when one of them slipped his cuffs and tried to take off the hood.

Which is a very, very clear threat – a man looking at you.

Necessary evil.

Everyone's a victim.

No doubt about that.

You get an education in that.

Injured parties on every side.

You weren't quite there and you didn't quite see it and were only informed at a later time of what occurred. No sounds were audible and no jokes were made.

No question.

You will go to the Pleasure Beach next.

It isn't a beach. It won't be a pleasure.

'Is it still the same? Still the same stuff?' He wants you to talk, unburden.

'Yeah, the same.'

'Searching? You just do office work and the searching? Do you still have to?'

'I search the women sometimes. Yes. And I do first aid. It's mainly admin, though, with the other Dorises.' A long time ago this was true and all that you were informed you'd be involved with and a source of contentment and a duty well performed.

'Admin?'

'Admin.'

At the Pleasure Beach you will be not able to meet your already-dead mother and your already-dead nan and your turned-back-to-being-younger father and they will not tour you about in another time, a further than hell and the moon and who you were and nailed underground already time when there were magical undercurrents that could pick you up clear like a prize in one of those grabber machines, drop you down safe in the slot and ready to be loved as was intended.

White tiles – a flat white with squares on it, like squared paper, the type you'd use for maths. When you think of it like that whatever happens becomes calmer, quiet, whatever you see.

Easy to hose down.

After the necessary evil.

Ask them questions, though, and the fuckers have nothing to say and they should say – stands to reason, if they'd actually fucking make an effort to help you, then it would stop.

Or not.

It has a purpose.

A not-clear purpose.

If there was none, that would be
That would be
You remember – very sharply remember – being in a
playground, your school playground, and you were skipping.
This day – mental – you were skipping and something caught
all of you, this craziness – one girl and then another, then
another, you didn't know who'd started it – nice girls and
the good sisters watching, bemused – it was like there'd been
this silent agreement – and everything else was just stopped
and you're bounding, covering ground – you've let go and
it feels, it feels, it feels – eventually all of you are covering
the ground and you're widening into a kind of circle until
your hands brush each wall and boundary fence and your
footfalls are loud and there's no talking, shouting, laughing,
only this movement that all of you have – wild with it –
arms swinging – dizzy with it – every one of you together
and this is what you have to do, this is wonderful – this is
most wonderful, this is being a big no one, a big everyone,
big happy and your worries gone and your body so alive
and unalone.

It's sort of what you'd wanted – to get that back. You'd
wanted to be one among many and safe in it – a bit of
searching females when required, paperwork, filing, honour,
having a laugh when possible. You wanted to give and get
respect, which was meant to be available.

'You have to pay to get in now.' His body is sad, the will
in it is deforming and soon he'll do something regrettable,
undignified.

'Where?'

'The Pleasure Beach – you pay to get in and then some
of the things are free and other stuff you pay again.'

You would like to hold his hand, suggesting compassion, but fingers are a difficulty. You cannot stand them any more – how they are both clever and delicate.

Explained very early – information which serves you well – like how to undertake the bulling of your boots – that real guardsman shine, cavalry shine, important and mind out for cracks – and more important, most important, is that you have the one mouth and two ears and so you listen and shut up, you listen and shut up and it is not your fault.

Except that was incorrect.

That was bollocks.

You shouldn't listen, because listening has effects.

You also shouldn't see.

And you shouldn't be present and an observer and you also shouldn't be a participant, which you can't help if you're there – you're out or in, no halfway – and you also shouldn't walk out of the room and leave it going on behind you and you shouldn't go far off and lie down on your bed while what's happening happens and what's going on goes on – there's no out, you're only in – you can still hear, like everyone can hear, but no one listens.

So you don't listen.

Can't go on if you listen.

It has to be like they sewed up your head, like you pulled the sack down over your head and you've pissed off out of it.

Missing.

You go missing.

You have to miss more.

Takes an effort.

The Effects of Good Government on the City

Is a problem.
But they say that you'll be fine.
Go to Cyprus, get forgetful, you'll be fine.
Think once you're out of Blackpool you'll be fine.

Run Catch Run

It couldn't last. Not this. There was no way it ever would have.

Never mind.

That's what you say when stuff buggers up – *never mind.* Simon's adults said it all the time. First there would be talking that fell into pieces and then retreats, fussing in more distant rooms and, after that, silences until one told the other *never mind.* This gave them something to do, beyond being helpless. Adults couldn't be helpless. They were, but they couldn't. But they were.

Never mind.

Simon wasn't minding.

He was sitting on the beach and not minding with the dog – his still-unnamed dog. They'd settled themselves on the cobbles as much as they could. It was that kind of beach. Uncomfortable. A seaside without sand. There weren't even any patches of little stones, or maybe gravel – you got nothing but these big, grey cobbles: lumpy when you sat, clacking and unsteady when you tried to walk. They made everybody look crippled and end up being slow, getting nowhere much.

Simon was hunched down a touch, his back to the far-away path, partly because he was warmer like that and partly as if he were hiding – which he was, only no one was looking for him, so that probably meant he wasn't. The looking produced the hiding, he knew that: without it you were only playing a game in your head.

And he knew about the opposite, too: hiding was the best way to get looked at. Simon had been hiding for two weeks. To be exact, he had kept on pretending to himself and playing a game in his head for sixteen days and now here was the truth, pressing at his ribs, searching. The feel of how things would turn out was already in his throat and sinking. Cold. By this evening, the inside of him would be uncovered and shown to be stupid. His mother would see. Everybody would see, including him.

Silly boy. Silly little boy. Could do better. Ought to. Must. *Never mind.*

The dog wasn't bothered, though. She was just breathing on his hand, which was nice for him and good. And she was much larger than on Monday. Yesterday, when she tried to bite the tennis ball, she couldn't manage because of having a too-small mouth, but today on the beach she'd caught it, held it and had been so pleased, crazy with having defeated it when it had seemed really that clever and puzzling before. Simon had known – because he knew things about his dog – that she was imagining a great huge forever and ever of chasing and bringing back and had found the idea so beautiful she had to shudder and give one big bounce. Then she'd stopped imagining and had run and run and been desperate with having to run more: catch, run, catch. Eventually, finally, she'd raced herself out, panted into a flop and so was – at the moment – warm and heavy on him and given up to sleep.

His dad had suggested she could be called Pat, which was a joke: Pat the dog. Simon didn't want to make his dog a joke.

He sneaked his finger along her muzzle – the silk and wiry tickle of her – and made her twitch with memories.

But he didn't want to wake her.

To the left of Simon – not close – a man was wedging a towel's corners under rocks and then balancing – one foot, the other – to undress. Woollen hat, parka, pullover, shirt, trousers, socks, he staggered them off and then paused in what was left: an onshore breeze and orange trunks. His skin was greyish and a sadness about the angles of him showed he was ashamed of himself and wasn't as fit as he had been and couldn't keep his stomach tucked flat. He stepped beyond the towel like someone intending to be athletic, but the cobbles foxed him and he slithered across the tricky slope before the sea, seemed to be hurt in his toes, visibly beaten. Eventually, he didn't stand up straight, simply rushed and staggered for the water, flailed into the dark rise of a wave.

The sections of shoreline to either side of this had notices which said their bits of sea weren't safe. Simon didn't swim anywhere in case he got lost, or swept to the dangerous parts. The current was strong. He could see it fighting the man, stealing his direction and making the bald top of his head mark time, or drift, while his arms tried to be powerful in changeable directions.

Simon hoped the man wouldn't start drowning. There were lifebelts back at the path, but the drawings that showed how to use them were confusing.

He looked down at his dog.

She did need a name.

Simon understood that when you're born, you're not called anything and then people study you and think of what would suit – how you are will tell them what to pick. There would have been a time when something about him said *Simon* and his parents noticed. That's what must have happened, because he wasn't named after somebody else – not a relative, or that – he was Simon, and Simon was him. Otherwise he couldn't feel right when he answered to it.

He wanted his dog to feel right when she answered to her name. For now, she would run to him if he whistled or clapped. He was careful not to say any words when he wanted her, in case she got confused about them and thought they were hers.

Whatever was chosen would have to be like her and what she was like was needle teeth and smooth pads to her paws – pink – and new in the world. The first time they'd walked outside, she'd been shaking, she'd wound in tight beside him and made him stumble. But she'd got excited, too, and tugged her leash and dashed at spaces in the air, or sniffed and yipped, which was almost the largest noise that she could make so far, and on the trip back they'd met a Labrador which was enormous, but slow, and his dog had flattened all the way down so the stranger dog couldn't touch her, or sniff her, or anything, but she'd been yipping up at it the whole while, so you were sure that she wasn't allowing herself to be bullied. She was brave. Simon had frowned and kept quiet and eventually the Labrador's owner had stopped smiling and talking and had gone, yanking the Labrador along behind.

Simon had picked up his dog when they were fine and alone again and had said happy things to her and smiled into the fur over her shoulders where it was loose and crumply.

Springer spaniel.

That's what she was.

Better than a Labrador. Neater.

And braver.

Much braver.

At the moment she was just happy, folded up neat and dozing inside the well of his crossed legs.

If she was touching Simon then she was happy. Simon also. That was how they were.

And if they were together and both awake, he would bend forward and slap his knees and she would barrel in against him and lift her paws on to his shins, which was supposed to be not allowed. She shouldn't jump up. That had been mentioned. He was choosing to allow it, though, because sometimes he wanted her to stretch her length against him, all there on tiptoe and with her tail wild about how excellent it was and her eyes finding his – looking, finding. She was very obedient normally and beginning to be trained. People should appreciate that.

The stones underneath him were draining his heat. His mother said if he was outside he ought to keep moving and warm and not in a dream. She worried when he was without her and warned him about not getting into cars, or talking to men or women he didn't know, about everything he wouldn't do anyway, because he wasn't an idiot.

He wasn't that kind of idiot.

Never mind.

Quite close by, a gull wandered and pecked into

shadows, stepping as badly and stupidly as everything else. It limped on, swaying when the wind cuffed it, clinging the grubby pink webs of its feet round the stones. No one was lovely here, or fast and easy – no one but his dog.

With a dog he would be protected.

They both would.

That was obvious.

She needed a rest currently because she was a puppy and that was all right and they could keep being like they should and having a play about for another hour. Then his dad would have finished talking to his mother and would want to tell Simon goodbye and go home and be with Pauline. After last time, Sandra hadn't come along. She'd only made not-good banana rolls for the trip and kissed his hair, which she hadn't done before and so she was useless at it and banged his head with her chin. She'd waved them goodbye. Simon had been in the passenger seat, although he'd wanted to sit in the back beside the dog's cage, because for his dog the cage meant a change was happening and that was mostly going to see the vet and so she'd be upset. Earlier in the morning, Simon had tried to explain that she wouldn't be meeting the vet, she'd be meeting a different house with the sea near it. The words wouldn't work, though – he hadn't expected they would – and when he tried again in the car he'd been loud because of the distance and speaking above the engine, and loud wasn't calm, it was shouting.

He'd been hoping that if he was calm and sounded it, then she would be the same. They were often the same. Except that she was too upset to hear him. She'd howled for the whole of the journey, which was her very loudest noise, her shouting, and fair enough when she believed that he ought to come and save her. Fair enough. She wasn't being bad. It had seemed like her own voice was causing her harm, like she was tearing. You could laugh about her, because she was being a baby, but that didn't mean it wasn't awful when you had to hear how scared she was. His dad yelled so that she would stop, but after that the howl got worse and really horrible.

They'd all been a bit odd when they'd arrived.

His mother was odd back at them and then turned round fast and headed for the kitchen. There was a silence that trailed from where she'd been standing, very thick and obvious, leading into the hall. Simon carried the cage and felt the strangeness of how it shifted when his dog moved inside. When he was close, his dog had gone quiet and he'd spoken to her gently about her being welcome home.

Simon spent holidays and some weekends with his father, but lived mainly in his mother's flat, which he told his dog was a house.

Really, both his parents lived in half-houses, which made sense, because when they didn't hate each other because of sex, they had lived in one whole house. Simon didn't like that everything was smaller since the separation – which was what came before a divorce – and his dad had no garden and at his mother's they had to share with the lady upstairs who owned all the flowers, which wasn't sharing – it was putting up with someone being greedy.

And his dad had Sandra in his halved house – up the stairs with the worn-out carpet and this is your room for when you come: wardrobe with a creaky door and sheets that smelled funny. Sandra made his dad scared. He would try and hide it, but that just meant that Simon would look and have to pretend he didn't see when his dad's face got frightened and sad. It was to do with kissing. After kissing. Or during. Not at first, but always it would happen. Like the fat man getting undressed and then being no use in the water, disappointing himself.

He was finished with trying to swim – the fat man – and creeping up to his towel, most of him red with the cold and his legs perhaps not exactly doing what he expected, due to being tired.

Simon watched.

The man didn't like being watched.

Simon watched more.

His dog snuggled and pushed, then smoothed back to stillness.

She could be perfectly, amazingly still. The moment before he bent to lift her she would drop into this peace, would be only waiting for him and peace. It tingled his fingers.

The man was unpeaceful, doubled over and his towel flapping round his legs as he fussed inside it and his wet trunks appearing, clinging down his shins. He'd still be wet when he put on his trousers. He hadn't been enjoying himself.

Adults didn't know how to enjoy anything. They did stuff and then wondered why they'd bothered. They couldn't decide what they wanted.

Simon's dad would think that they ought to all squash on the sofa in the lounge at his place and watch DVDs, but it was awkward. There'd be proper adventures and good bits in the films, but then the top man and top woman would have sex, or at least kissing. And Simon would be caught between his dad – who'd miss breaths during the kisses – and Sandra – who was made of bigness and curves and trying not to laugh. The three of them would have to stay put until the sex stopped. Then his dad would ask if anyone wanted tea, or crisps, or a can of something and he'd go off and be sort of hiding, while Simon and Sandra pretended that he wasn't, and then he'd come back and kiss both of them on the cheek, but still be not happy.

Simon's dad was with Sandra because of sex.

His mum was not with anyone because of sex.

Simon knew sex made you scared: scared and sad. And angry as well.

Sex made you want to go and want to stay, which was impossible. It wasn't a way of getting enjoyment.

Simon felt his dog shift again. He looked at her and she looked back, gave a broad yawn. Before she could close her mouth again he set his thumb between her teeth and so she gave him a tiny, hot, secret bite. They did that – it had a meaning for them.

She coiled, uncoiled and scrambled until she was set and organised and on her feet, ready for goings-on, braced. Simon stood – his legs cold where she wasn't any more – and threw her ball, saw her leap into a half-spin and pursue it. They were heading away from the fat man and his troubles. Simon decided to hate him and gave him a farewell stare. The man stumbled. Simon wondered if being ignored would make someone stumble as much as being stared at, but didn't check.

Next he wondered why people would be naked with each other and do what they did when they were so ugly.

Or, after the first time, it wasn't clear to him how they'd keep on. Simon knew that he'd never be able to, wouldn't want to. He wouldn't be that kind of idiot, either.

He rubbed his hands together. In movies and on telly, people did that to show they were cold.

He was.

Forgot his gloves.

Like his own kind of idiot.

It would take twenty minutes to get home, which wasn't long. He could add another ten or fifteen minutes with dodging about, but there wouldn't be much point.

Up ahead, birds were fretting in a mob not far offshore. Simon slipped and trudged closer until he could see they were mainly terns – the spiky, small ones, sharp wingtips – hovering and peering and then throwing themselves into the water like something angry. Like being furious. They would spring up to the surface again with thin silver trembles of fish in their beaks. So there must be a shoal trapped underneath and they were raiding it, killing. Bobbing by itself was a tall, round-headed bird, pale and noticeable. Simon wasn't sure what it was until it started a long, clumsy flap across the wave tops and then eased into the air: mournful, winding upwards, huge and slow. A young gannet. Which shouldn't be here. They were for cliffs and up-high places. Its problem was that it was young and didn't know what it should do.

The dog rattled up and dropped the ball, which Simon threw without caring about where, so that it splashed into the shallows. He was concentrating on the gannet as it wheeled in a long, cream reach. He saw the wings hinge, swing and tuck themselves back until the bird was brought to a clean point before it sleeked into the sea and disappeared. It stayed under for ages, was better than the others and strong against the current and okay.

His dog was snapping at the waves, baffled, eyeing the ball as it wagged and teased, floating. She didn't want to get her feet wet: she'd never had wet feet before.

Some of the terns grew anxious.

The gannet emerged to sway on the waves and eat. It belonged in the water and in the air. It was an expert. Simon and his dog were just land things, which seemed limiting, although Simon could think better than a bird's thinking. He could think that he was fast in the brain and cleverer than any type of animal probably. He made plans. Which was why he knew he had to tell his parents about the gannet. It would rescue everything. Simon would stand here as he was against the salt wind and he would concentrate and teach himself how to get correctly excited about the bird and how to pass on wildlife information. Then he would go home and be what got their attention. His dad was interested in nature and his mum wanted him to have the benefit from lots of good experiences, and the gannet story would satisfy them both.

But his dog wanted the ball, worried at the shoreline, yipped and pounced, and either this or his coming to make her quiet lost him the gannet. It stretched and pounded back into flight and turned from them both, whiter and whiter as it shrank, left.

So there wouldn't be enough to say.

This was his dog's fault, but Simon's, too.

His dog scampered to him, put her paws against his shins to greet him and he shut his eyes for a moment. Then he looked at her, found her, let her find him. She whined, because he wasn't rubbing her ears, or fussing at her yet. He drew back a step and she let him go, before sitting – perhaps surprised – in front of him, liver-and-white and brave and wonderful.

He kicked her.

Never mind.

The worst thing he had ever done.

Never mind.

The one short cry she made hit into him and then she was quiet and crouching and batting against him and her head dropped and her tail uncertain and she touched him and touched him and touched him and he knelt and held her and whispered he was sorry and held her more and rubbed his face next to hers and let her lick it.

Never mind.

His one hand was cupped under her ribs, and the whole of who she was and would be was in there and was moving and was all for him. She would let him do anything and was his.

Never mind.

And he was hers.

And he would take her back home with nothing to defend them and nothing to break his mother's attention and to stop her explaining that his father should never have bought a dog and that presents as big as that should be discussed and they couldn't keep it, they couldn't afford it – vet's bills, food, mess, equipment – and his father couldn't afford it, either. And his father would agree. His dad wasn't steady and would fall when his mother pushed.

A dog wasn't possible. It would be decided. His mother

wouldn't give them a chance, wouldn't spend the evening with his dog and be patient and find how they could be.

Simon had known this.

Never mind.

He'd been right when he didn't give his dog a name.

A Thing Unheard-of

The thing is, you know they'll be thinking much the same. They will be planning some version of your plan and it's only a matter of time and so forth before they get into action, begin taking steps. And their steps will be very similar to your steps, the ones which you would take, so you're fully forewarned and yet still vulnerable, because they'll have many plans, some more and some less dreadful, and you'll never be able to guess which one they'll pick. You can't pre-empt that kind of galloping inspiration and perhaps you shouldn't. And perhaps you'll agree with their final decision – it might turn out that you can't distinguish it from the one that you would have deployed, had you got in first. Your opposite number is, you're wholly certain, in general and in the particular not your opposite, which is an issue, a real trial. You know what they know and vice versa, and your mutual knowing cannot be undone and your anxieties and counter-measures therefore escalate as theirs undoubtedly do, too. You feel at risk from them, as they must do from you, which means they will act and therefore so must you, because their risks will generate actions which cause your risks, or your fears will cause actions which will summon their duly risk-propagating response. It's all very unpredictable, but also guaranteed. It could be nothing else.

And, most likely, you're now both thinking in total unison – *I will make conversation when we meet and I will say, 'The coffee here's good.' That's what I'll begin with. Straight after good morning or good afternoon, or whatever is appropriate.*

Morning would be best: it's the least emotionally charged time of day and will be brighter and have a sense of moving on, of futures and being uplifted.

Although it can also produce an atmosphere of having just left one's bed. That scent. The good one.

But afternoons could get cantankerous and evenings are too mellow and unfurling and nights are clearly a threat.

The coffee here's good.

The coffee here's good this morning.

But why would you decide to say that? Why on earth? Who would that mean you'd become? It would turn you into somebody misleading, casual, and a person who'll seem cruel in retrospect. You don't want that. You're not cruel.

They're not cruel, either.

You have faith they wouldn't choose to be.

But they might, nonetheless, have found it necessary.

Anyway, you're fussy about coffee and haven't been some-where with a really good brew available in years, not with coffee worth a positive mention, so remarking upon it randomly in some mediocre venue would be weird, if not laughable, and this won't be an issue even, because, as you consider it thoroughly, a meeting at a café would be inap-propriate. You've enjoyed that sort of niceness before, but you shouldn't again. It could lead you astray. Once you'd arrived, you might start relaxing, even though you'd be feeling lousy, and then you'd brush fingers while you chat with them and share opinions and none of it would end at the intended end. So you won't go to a café in the first place.

And visiting each other's homes would be an act of violence.

You can't.

You won't.

You couldn't.

You won't go anywhere.

You won't meet.

You are unable.

You shouldn't trap yourself in a position where you see their mouth, study their mouth and the movement of their lips and the terrible softandgentleness of everything: the dark and lovely, clever softening.

It would be a disaster.

Hi.

Likewise, every possible form of address – any speaking when you're together – would be wrong.

How are you?

What does that mean?

What are the implications?

You're a person who weighs implications and so are they, and that's a factor to consider while you plan. Despite the unfortunate circumstances, you want to be kind and do this right. They will do too. And there's the question of respecting the other party who's also involved and who has no way to alter this and neither can you.

I just can't.

I'm not sure any more.

I was never sure.

But I'm sure I can't.

And meanwhile you, there's you and you were, you really,
you absolutely – I absolutely – in all of the ways I would
like to – in all of the ways I would like

But I

But I

But I

But I

Phone would be better.

Getting clear of the same room, or building, or street
would seem better, easier.

Much.

Much worse, if you're being frank. Only a moral bankrupt would attempt to make this tidy over the phone.

Only a moral bankrupt would view this in terms of
being *tidy*, and you're not that. Your terminology was a
mistake. The permanent grief that you have in the muscles
along your forearms since you can't remember when is
destroying your vocabulary and you scramble for phrases as
if you're abroad somewhere inexplicable and scary. Sometimes
your head is stuffed with no more than noises and you're
afraid that, if you tried to speak, an animal mess would be
the best you'd manage. You'd squeal and be undignified.
There's also a long, anxious tendon, or connective something, a strained nerve, that stings when you reach to the
left, or roll over at night – your sleep is, naturally, ruined
– and there's a sense that when you swallow you come inap-
propriately close to drowning.

I'm not drowning.

I don't want to.

Your mind is unworkable and over-full.

Perhaps theirs is equally busy with aches and scrambles.

I could make a call, though. I could write down the points I should cover and be reassured and then deliver them presentably.

But if you phone, you'll hear them breathing, precisely as they might when they're skin-tight to your cheek and they find out the secrets along your neck and are warm and dense and interesting – they fit so much motion against you, demonstrate such a burden of potential, even when they're at rest. There are other people who are communicative as fence posts when you hold them: truly numbing, somehow. As if they had gone and left something dead, propped up in the space behind them. Or there are those who are peculiarly, or almost unnervingly, a horrible shape when touched. They're like badly packed duffel bags with absurdist contents. You don't like them. They are acquaintances. Or less.

Your life has uncomfortable requirements, one of them apparently that you should hold the unholdable as part of many low-grade social interactions. Comprehensive contact is the fashion currently. How this has come about is beyond you. You didn't ask for it.

You ask for very little.

Historically, this is true.

Hi, I was calling to

Hi is better than hello. It's smaller.

Hi.

Or hey. Hey delivered as a smoother version of hi. A dab of sound.

They will recognise your voice.

Even from that dab.

They'll know it's you.

They will know you are you, but quite possibly misunderstand what that implies.

Hey.

I was not calling to say that you are endless information. My palms against your back have touched unmistakably the way that you're built out of shouts and whispers, croons – you have these areas that croon.

You have sweet shapes.

You have places about you that shift my senses and make me have to understand your heats as flavours. You lead to kissing. Always.

You lead to blatant inadequacy and the fear of death, and the kissing blesses all of that away. You unharm me.

And I will never get used to the times when your breath splinters, or to the necessity of cradling. It is correct to cradle you.

There have been times when I have heard you and wanted only to run and cure whatever was wrong, whatever could be wrong, whatever might be wrong.

I am not calling to say that.

So I won't say that.

It would be, to a degree – not that you're ungrateful – an inventory of things you've never asked for.

Hey.

I couldn't predict what you would give me.

And you'd have to agree, I didn't ask for it.

You'll only tell them the one thing, small sound.

Hey.

After which they will have recognised your voice and then they'll want to chat and you'll need to be savage and get in there first like a cold-calling salesman.

Doing this will be vile. Completely. How completely vile of you.

And thereafter they'll have their own points they need to make and comments, of course. You will end up having a discussion, conversing.

You're already upset, as it is.

So when they start talking you'll really be in trouble.

Hey, I

You won't make a call, then. Not any kind of call – not ringing to leave them a message and ducking the issues arising, which would be cowardly to a degree that you might not survive. You might remain despicable to yourself for the duration after that.

You've established – because you intend to live decently, always have – this habit of testing your actions in advance. You ask – *will doing this leave me with permanent regrets?*

It's a not unreasonable question.

In this case, simply dumping your decision as a fuzzily recorded message, talking when you're sure that they can't answer back, would be impossible. It would be too wrong.

Dear.

A letter defeats itself from the very start.

Dear.

It would be like confessing what you no longer should.

To Whom It May Concern:

Which would mean pretending you can't name them and do not hold them dear.

You do hold them.

Dear God.

To whom we will offer no prayers, because we neither deserve them, nor understand how they would work.

No letter.

No.

No here are your fingers where mine have rested and not been at rest, where they've howled, to be more accurate, in the usual manner for you for you for dear you, tendrils of darkness and liquid wishes rippling along the little bones, slowing minorly at each joint and at each thrum where you have previously kissed and the paper was warm when I left it, warm where I paused, where my skin was waiting, and tends to wait and has learned to wait and croons – I like to think it croons and you have found this in me, touched and heard this in my skin – and if you read what I put for you in ink, old-fashioned ink, it will show you the blurs and hesitations in my hope and the shrinking when I get uneasy and my horrible desire to push through and reach you where you will be, where you will be holding my mind in this, my most soft things in this, and you'll be fragile there and breathing delicate and not enough loved because I have not enough love because there is not enough love because you make sure that my self and my love are both not enough. I mean to be more, but I am not.

Believe me, I didn't ask for that.

And no one meant to give it.

You do realise.

And a letter would be inappropriate, because you shouldn't continue to be opened and unfolded in that manner, it would give the wrong impression.

Dear.

Very dear.

You could instead consider the many electronic options which will keep you eternally untouched. Clean.

But you can't type some absence or presence of light across a screen and hope to send it without your self-esteem intervening.

It would be like wrapping your note round a stone and then throwing it in through their window.

I just wanted to say.

There is no easy way to say.

I have to say.

You might hit them, hurt them.

But you're not a vandal.

I'm contacting you in this way to tell you I'll never contact you again.

You're not the person this would seem to make you.

I would love to. I did love to.

You're not the person you seem to be when you're with them.

You're not that frail little list of attempts to do better than you have and be better and act better when eventually, you realise, you won't. You'll be disappointing. You'll do worse.

I think it would be better if you could go.

I think I would be better if you could go.

I think I could revert to being worse in a way that would be better if you could go.

Please go.

It will make no sense to tell them how much this appals you.

Unless they are also appalled, which you suspect, and

which means that soon they will appal you, which will be completely unbearable and when you ask for their support you won't, and shouldn't, get it.

You can't let that happen. You can't wait for that to happen. Not any longer.

You're worn out.

You're worn out and away.

Very dear.

Your only realistic option is to do nothing and to say nothing, to answer nothing and eventually they'll work out what's going on and, by then, they will hate you enough for matters to be simpler.

You don't want them to have any difficulty. You really, really don't.

So very dear.

Not at any time.

This Man

There's this man and he's telling you a story. Only he's not.

You're sitting together on uneasy, weatherproof chairs. He's dragged both of them out here to benefit from the sun, hauled out the table too and nobody from the café made any objections. He seemed authoritative when he said, 'First good day of the year. How lovely.' And he left a pause beyond *lovely* during which he did not look at you.

Although you were also not looking – not looking at him – you had a clear sense of *his* not looking. You could feel it. If he'd asked what it was like, you could have told him – *it's like a tender hollowness, or some odd colour in the fall of light.*

He didn't, of course, ask.

You didn't, of course, tell him.

But you were paying attention.

You still are.

He'd then added, 'Good' rather quietly and with a kind of helplessness, after which he'd rallied and re-repositioned the seats. Something about his movements during these proceedings had suggested a happy assurance – there might be many areas of doubt, but here he was certain: sitting face-to-face wasn't going to work. And anyone would have advised that side-by-side was a touch eccentric, if not reminiscent of pensioners waiting to die on a seaside bench – the type local councils fix near pleasant views to memorialise other pensioners who once also liked to sit near pleasant views.

You can imagine – are unable not to – a future within which you might lean against him as you consider your arthritis, or his replacement hip, and how the wind would ruffle what's left of anything and make you love him all the more, while he loves you back to a comparable degree. Or maybe you'd just eat sandwiches in a bitter and familiar pause and then go home to hate each other for another decade. It's not uncommon.

Which is inappropriate. You're on a first date. Why picture the brownish parka in which you apparently think he'll take decrepit holidays? Why conjure up domestic horrors and spats over too much pickle that will have dampened the nasty bread? Why assume you'll have nasty bread?

It's not that you believe this nonsense – *'I can't abide pickle, I've told you. And that bread's nasty. Where's my pills?'* – it's more that you'd rather anticipate fictional disasters than deal with your awareness of how many true things can go wrong.

'They'll bury you in that parka.'

'I'd like to see them try.'

This man isn't a pensioner, or in a parka. He dresses nicely, like a person who understands his own shape. You appreciate it. Without looking. Without looking much.

And he'd understood the shape he'd required from his

surroundings before he'd finally let you sit. He'd needed the chairs at ninety degrees to each other: enough to keep you close across one corner of the table, but not too close. He hadn't wanted you too close.

So maybe you'd made him ambivalent from the beginning.

Or maybe your date is evasive – or else considerate, shy, romantic, a tease, anal-retentive, insanely controlling, or otherwise strange.

Your mind kicks and shies through a range of distracting suggestions: he might be someone who's used to cramped tables, possibly keen on camper vans, works in a cubicle, poker player in miniature casinos, brought up on boats, lives in a shed.

None of this is true.

But, equally, you're not too sure what is.

You do not know him, this man. He is practically a stranger.

And you can't think why he chose to see you here: at a concrete theatre complex with an equally concrete café and this concrete square baking airlessly in front where there is no one – no one but this man and you. The other exterior tables and wiser diners and unadjusted chairs are over by the building. They nestle in its shadows, are thickest towards the angle where two wings meet. Ninety degrees again.

Four ninety degrees, to be technical. You're in a square – it's square.

Perhaps he has a thing for corners.

Or else he likes display. You do feel that you have been forced to become one half of an event. Inside the café, people are eating ahead of a matinee, grabbing a coffee, studying their programmes, chatting in a manner that suggests they have made good choices in life and are about to savour something enriching and not to just anyone's taste. Outside, there's you and this man and what amounts to an audience. Every now and then someone lifts their head in the shade, stops talking, glances over and sees – *this couple meeting, this couple having lunch, this man telling this woman a story.*

Only he's not.

He isn't really saying anything.

He began with the stutter and falter of, 'Sorry. Excuse me. I'll just . . . Ah. Well. Hang on.' And there was the minor chaos you guess that he always draws up and around him: the furniture moving and the scamper back and forth as he fetched superfluous napkins, another spoon, the glass for your apple juice, a glass of ice for the glass for your apple juice, some pepper in a handful of sachets which remain untouched. Then he sat, swallowed audibly and began, running off through longer and longer sentences, looping them forward while he showed you the flinch of his hands, the over-vigorous illustration of salient and mildly amusing points. All his details blur and fade, though, and he reaches no conclusions. He tangles and frequently breaks his own thread, and you feel that his general rush of words amounts to a hedge, a fence, energetic smoke. They are the cover that he ducks behind.

He was the one who asked to meet you, but he's now in hiding. He is even crouching to a tiny degree, shoulders tensed, as he tells you the first coat he bought that was properly expensive had actually been a knock-off with fraudulent seams that unravelled and he'd also bought a second-hand stove that harboured almost fatal electrical flaws. You haven't expressed any interest in fashion, or stoves, or very unwise decisions. Before this, he half-finished an anecdote about cats which seemed intended to be funny, but wasn't. Perhaps if he'd made it to the end.

His being so far away and yet here makes you lonely.

You stare at your lasagne, which is ugly and has congealing historical layers, like a starchy lump of cliff – not something you can eat.

There's a plate of allegedly Moroccan casserole in front of him. It hasn't been attempted.

This isn't having lunch with him, this is visiting lunch with him.

You should have brought your own food to ignore – bad cheese and wet pickle, nasty bread – it would have been cheaper.

'*I hate pickle.*'

'*Well, I didn't know that.*'

'*Well, I've been telling you for thirty-seven years.*'

Start as you'd rather not have to continue.

You remember arriving early – the more important the occasion, the earlier you'll be – and then having to wander, wait, lean against the warmed bulk of the embankment wall.

It felt good, reliable, relaxing.

Not like this.

You'd looked down at the retreated tide and the narrow drifts of dirty sand it had abandoned. They made you think *this lets it seem that somewhere underneath the grey and the burden of straight edges, unnatural angles, London could still be a living thing and might simply shrug one random*

morning and crack its surfaces and let fundamental elements
– sand, rock, water – run loose.

Which might just have been something to consider rather than considering this man and your imminent meeting, or it might have been caused by the slowed and silvered air and the city being briefly turned to silhouettes, lacework and bright prospects. There was a sweetness when you breathed, as if leaves were waking somewhere out of sight.

You were happy. Unmistakably.

You didn't quite believe that you were happy because of him, but could have been persuaded.

Then he arrived – quick and with a slight flail in his limbs, a vaguely tangential approach – and his nervousness made you nervous, as if he had identified a threat you couldn't place.

They're worse now, your nerves, because you are so firmly by yourself. Still, he would do you no harm. You can tell. This is rare in men, in people, and is therefore attractive and it makes you miss him.

You allow yourself – *I miss him.*

And you watch the side of his face as he laments the failures of professional carers, and dentists in particular. His own glass of apple juice is raised, but he does no more than peer at it for an instant and put it down again, being unable to either halt or drink.

Apart from your bottle of apple juice, you've got water and a pot of tea. You have to suppose you expected to be thirsty. And then there's the glass of melting ice.

You're not thirsty.

You pour out some juice and add ice, cube by cube, so slowly that it hurts your fingertips.

It may be that you miss him less and are at the edge of being bored.

You pour out some tea, add ice to that.

He forgot to bring milk and so did you. No way you're going to mention it now and send him haring off again. You'll have your tea iced and wish for lemon, but not ask for that either.

You're not exactly listening any more.

His throat, his neck – you want to touch them with the chill of your fingers, find out if they're as soft and private as they seem, as delicate. The sudden necessity of this prickles in your hands, it nags, and you're no longer bored. It could be that you're irritated. You don't know.

Then his knee – *dunt* – politely – *dunt* – rests for a breath against yours – *dunt* – withdraws – *dunt* – returns and stays, grazes up and then down and then stays with a pressure which is nearly an absence and therefore aches.

He is – still talking, still focused beyond your right shoulder – with you.

You do not move.

You are – the concrete around you visibly in tiny motion, every surface changing beneath the heat – with him.

He is with you.

You are with him.

At least, this could be the case.

He is describing his mother – his mother up a set of steps and being scared to change a light bulb – that reaching up, angled head and unsteady hands, lifted eyes, the risk of a fall in return for illumination. He makes it real. He takes away his knee. Whatever he's recalling makes him sad and his eyes, when they find yours, are fast and open and right

here and have a shine of pain in them and a deeper intention you can't grasp before it goes.

And now it's all silent.

Miles off, years off, it could be that you can hear other
voices, meaningless voices, and the stir of the city, an aircraft
hanging in the distance – this doesn't matter.

The silence continues.

You have no idea what to do.

He nods. He sips his apple juice. His eyes become ordinary and cautious before they refocus beyond you. Softly,
he describes a trip to Dublin and you reach your fingers as
far as his arm and you touch it, when you hadn't anticipated
that you would. To be accurate, you don't notice that you've
moved until the cloth of his jacket is warm against you,
those one-two-three-four-and-the-thumb little areas of you.
At the same time, you realise you're not being comforting
because you're too late. Your gesture will seem like an
unwilling afterthought. He sort of turned to you, tried you,
was possibly upset, possibly about his mother, and you've
demonstrated how you won't support him, won't help until
he doesn't need it.

You've made a mistake.

Not a big one.

But personal situations like this – slightly undefined,
barely begun – are fragile and it seems he is quite unforgiving,
because after you withdraw your hand, his shoulders drop
and the Dublin excursion ends with, '. . . anyway. Where
was I . . .?' Something about him seems to have given up.

He prods the casserole with his spoon. He no longer
appears to be nervous, simply dismayed by unappealing food.

While he makes himself eat, you hammer together

remarks on the day and the river, let them go at intervals and rearrange areas of your lasagne.

You remove its corners.

But that only makes more.

If an observer were to glance over here again they would see – *acquaintances at lunch, acquaintances in the same place, the mutually restless gestures that suggest both parties will finish shortly and go away.*

Which is all right.

Really.

It is.

You don't absolutely need another friend, but he would be fine in that capacity. You could be content with that. Probably. An occasional coffee – no more lunches – could happen. Without the anxiety over whether you'll seem presentable, or sensible, or amusing, or lovable, or repeatable, or anyone significant, you could enjoy yourself. You could chat.

Or else you could not chat, as it turns out, because although you can feel yourself sinking into friendship, there is currently no conversation. This man is staring mutely towards the wide brightness of the water and the far bank and you aren't inclined to interrupt him. It seems there is nothing you can offer to beat the view.

Under other circumstances you might suggest fetching desserts, or getting more drinks – the ones you have being too cold, too hot, too unintoxicating, too incorrect. But you'd basically rather not, because it's obvious he'll make his excuses and refuse you. Having worked this through in your mind and therefore avoided being humiliated, you somehow already are.

You suspect you may have to be angry with him soon as a matter of sheer self-defence, and meanwhile there's no hesitancy left to prevent you from facing him, shifting your chair from its perfect location – you regret this, but he doesn't notice – and truly seeing at him.

Whatever could have formed between you is gone and over, but nevertheless you study him, what he is. This man.

And he is completely at rest and so it's plain, this truth you didn't find but should have – *he is beautiful.*

Sometimes he can't hide it.

And this information repositions everything – *dunt* – the chairs, table, concrete, city, river, sky, and makes them expressions of emptiness.

'So . . .' He stretches, rubs his hand at the back of his neck and frowns. 'Yes.' Gives you a bland smile. 'Time to go. I think. I think time to go.' After which he stands and you stand with him.

There is a point at the embankment – it arrives with an immense rapidity – where he must head left for his car and you must head right for the Underground, or for a walk across the bridge, or else a longer journey to exhaust yourself, break up through Westminster and into Soho, further, or else aim for Chelsea, for the World's End, and keep on going until it's dark and you are done.

You are very tired of being disappointed.

You'll get over it, be cheerier tomorrow, but standing in the sunlight with this man you're not over it yet.

You haven't taken his hand because the idea of shaking it goodbye makes you too sad.

And here are his shoes. You are evidently staring at his shoes. They are quite ugly. Like you.

'Okay. Okay.' This man who is not telling you a story. 'Okay.' But repeating one word for no particular reason. 'Okay.' Until he leans down and you can't help but look, it is natural to look, and he's here and increasingly close and then brings you a kiss.

This kiss.

He kisses with a pressure which is nearly an absence and therefore aches.

You kiss him back.

You do not kiss as if you are friends.

You do not kiss as if you are acquaintances.

You kiss, both of you, back and soft and back and soft and back.

You kiss each other back.

This kiss.

You do not know him, this man. He is practically a stranger. Only he's not.

Acknowledgements

Acknowledgements are due to the editors of the following:

Elsewhere (Edinburgh International Book Fair anthology), *Freedom* (Amnesty International anthology), *Granta*